A BODY IN THE BALLROOM

LADY ELLEN INVESTIGATES

KELLY MASON

LITTLE ORCHARD PRESS

For Liz Lane

Thank you

CHAPTER 1

"**W**ould you do me the honour of a dance?" Major Fitzwilliam asked after the host announced a waltz. It was the longest sentence I'd heard the Major utter during the few days I'd come to know him.

We were spending an evening in the smoky ballroom of The Grand Hotel and I hesitated. The poor man was holidaying alone, and whilst I would have preferred not to dance with him, I felt sorry for the fellow. He was old enough to be my father, and was a recent widower. He smiled waiting for my reply and touched his large moustache.

"Go on, Ellen," Lottie said as she sat down, panting from a rather energetic dance she'd shared with her sweetheart Sebastian.

The young man beamed at her as he also took his seat. "I'm having the most fun, and it's your turn now,

Ellen." He pulled Lottie by the hand and sat close beside her.

"I'd love to," I said to Major Fitzwilliam. I smiled at him as I rose from my chair. He led me to the floor with his head held high.

We were soon moving around the dance floor to 'Fascination' by Fermo Dante Marchetti. The Major was rather rigid in his movements, which was not surprising considering he was senior in years.

"Alice loved a waltz," he said, referring to his late wife. "We never mastered much else."

"It's one of my favourites also," I said, although I felt a lump form in my throat as I had waltzed to this particular piece of music on my wedding day. "Leonard and I danced often, when he was on leave from the war." My mind flashed back to my late husband. In his arms, I'd felt so loved, so completely his. It still seemed wretched, even after more than six years of widow-hood, that we would not spend our entire lives together. It was then that an image of Captain Ernest Hamilton snaked into my mind. A man I had become close to over recent months. *Could I ever feel the same way about him as I did about Leonard?* I thought. We'd spent much time together, from the spring of 1924 and through the summer. It was now early September. I pushed the vision of Hamilton away. It would be foolish to allow my heart to run away with itself over what had been a flirtation. *Or was it more?* I thought. It was difficult to know as we'd not explicitly discussed our friendship.

As I moved around the floor with the Major, I glanced at the other dancers. The hotel ballroom appealed to the mature guests, whilst the younger generation chose to socialise off the hotel grounds in the various jazz bars. The few younger guests that joined the older guests in the ballroom, such as Lottie and Sebastian, stood out from the crowd – especially during the more energetic dances when the dance floor was not so populated. I felt rather on the young side myself in the ballroom, and I was approaching thirty.

The host dancers passed us. They looked so completely graceful together. It was apt that we were dancing to a French number, considering the host himself was from the country. Michel Blanc held his fair-haired partner as if she was the only woman in the room. Her head was leaned back much further than the other female dancers, and she wore a daring dress revealing her bare back, the skirt so full that it ballooned out as she turned. She changed dresses throughout the evening depending on the style of dance. I watched the couple over Fitzwilliam's shoulder as they appeared to glide around the room, taking much longer strides than the rest of us. It was wonderful to watch and indeed brought me from my melancholy mood.

Fitzwilliam caught me gazing at them. "Beautiful."

Once the waltz had concluded, we returned to our table. The female host left the room for what I guessed was another dress change.

At our table, as well as Lottie and Sebastian were

the Simpson sisters who had joined us. They too were much older than us, but not as old as the Major and I placed them in their fifties. They were extremely entertaining company and were constantly smiling. Nelly was the slimmer of the two with a quiet voice, and Betty had a round friendly face, was extremely talkative and had an eye for the Major. They both wore matching gold-rimmed glasses with diamanté details on them. Their grey hair was styled as if they found a look they liked in 1910 and stuck with it. They wore dated clothes with skirts that brushed the floor – these spinsters appeared to be caught in a moment in time, in the clothes of their youth. The inquisitive part of me wondered what had happened that set their lives in stone, but I guessed it was likely to be an earlier war, and they were clutching onto a time before it happened. Each sat with the Major between them. They had clearly taken him under their wings.

"You looked beautiful dancing together," Betty said.

"Why don't you dance with the Major?" I asked.

Betty fanned herself. "Goodness, no. I'm not good enough."

"You should dance," Lottie said. "You're both very fit. Not at all like usual old ladies."

"Betty and Nelly are not old ladies," I interjected with a nervous laugh. Lottie was still learning her social awareness. I had plucked her from a role as a maid at a nearby hotel and made her my assistant, and she was still learning etiquette.

"But we are old," Nelly said with a small smile. "But thank you, dear, for the compliment."

Betty exchanged a smile with Fitzwilliam. I looked to the Major and wondered whether there could possibly be a romance between himself and Betty. Both sisters had told us they'd never married. I wondered sometimes, as I glanced at the spinsters, whether I would still be single in my fifties. I pushed yet another thought of Hamilton out of my mind.

"You could take lessons," Sebastian said to Betty.

"Michel gives private lessons on a Sunday evening," I added. "I've been considering attending one myself, as a refresher, or to maybe learn how to dance one of the more modern dances, such as the Charleston."

"It's too late for that," Betty said with a nervous laugh.

"You danced that waltz so well," Nelly said to me. "I'm sure you don't require lessons, my lady," she added with a neat smile. The sisters did seem to be rather enamoured by me. I presumed it was because of my title.

"Agreed," the Major said, relighting a cigar which he'd extinguished earlier in the evening. He then gave in to a bout of coughing, and placed his cigar in the ash tray as he reached for his handkerchief.

Betty nodded towards Michel as he whisked his partner, now dressed in a red dress, around the floor. "He's so skilled. Maybe we should learn. It would be nice to dance with the Major." She smiled shyly at him.

"Absolutely," he said with rosy cheeks.

As Michel passed by again, I remembered as a child visiting with my papa, peering through the doors of the ballroom, wishing that one day I would dance around the room with a handsome man.

"Michel and Pearl are the perfect couple," Lottie said.

"Had a few turns with Pearl," the Major said. "Like dancing with a feather."

"It's her last night," Betty said.

"Is she leaving?" Sebastian asked.

"She's landed herself a job in the chorus of a new Broadway show." Betty leaned forward. "It's back in America, that's where she comes from."

"It's called Lady, Be Good," Nelly added.

"She misses her family," Betty said. "We were talking to her earlier, weren't we Major."

"Certainly were."

"America's a big place," Nelly said.

"Vast," the Major added.

"I'd love to go to America," Lottie said.

"One day, we shall," Sebastian said to her, clutching her hand and giving her a broad smile.

"Have you been to America, my lady?" Betty asked.

"No, I've travelled throughout Europe and visited India, but not to the Americas."

"Maybe Ernest can take you," Lottie said with a smile. "We could all go together."

"He's far too busy," I said with a nervous laugh. "Captain Hamilton will be travelling to Cairo soon." My heart sank as I listened to my own words. He'd only broken the news to me that morning by letter – that he would be gone from England for many weeks. He'd attended to business in Bristol, which had then taken him onward to London, and I'd not seen him since we'd returned to Branden Bay. I had the feeling that I'd allowed myself to become too fond of him. Indeed, he was the first thing I thought of when I awoke and the last when I laid my head on my pillow. I had a fondness for him and found that my heart always beat a little faster when I was in his presence. I was embarrassed by that. A grown woman consumed by romantic thoughts. But as much as I dismissed my feelings as foolish, I longed to see him before he set sail, to consider whether this was a simple flirtation or whether there was a chance it could become something more akin to love. But I was unsure of his sailing date, or whether we would meet again before that time.

"What will Captain Hamilton be doing in Cairo?" Sebastian asked.

"He now has his own security company and will be guarding rare artefacts," I said. He'd also told me in his letter that it was a lucrative area, and that he could build a business to provide jobs for other men. Reading between the lines, I had felt that he wanted to impress me. I'd written back and told him how proud I was, yet secretly I would have preferred him not to be quite so ambitious when that ambition would take him away from me.

"Ooh, here comes Michel," Betty said, adjusting her gold-rimmed glasses as he reached our table.

"Can I have the pleasure of this dance?" Michel Blanc said as he outstretched his hand to me. His French accent was thick, as if he made no effort with his pronunciation of the English language.

"Oui, j'aimerais beaucoup danser avec toi." I replied in his native tongue, letting him know that I would love to dance with him.

He smiled but remained silent.

As I rose from my chair, I felt a little embarrassed. I had yet to dance with the host and as he took my hand, I told him in French that I was a little rusty. Again, he simply smiled as if not at all put off or worried that I may not be capable of keeping up with the steps. As we passed the band, he nodded at them and they began to play a tango. He spun me around, pulling me close against his torso. Normally, I would have protested. I considered the man too forceful, but a fire came to the fore, ignited by the music and a memory of dancing the tango with Leonard. I was sure Michel was used to seducing and dominating women. I could tell by the way his eyes bore into mine. I knew I could tango, I just had to rediscover the steps.

Michel's hand settled on my back and I allowed him to lead me along the floor. I moved as best I could and tried to follow his lead but my body tensed. *Come on, remember,* I told myself. As I recalled the steps, I battled the memories of when I last danced with Leonard. I worried that if I let my mind return fully to that time, it would be accompanied by a rush of sadness. *You can do it,* I told myself as my heart thudded in my chest. Not only did I want to recall this dance I'd loved, I was also beginning to dislike Michel Blanc. He was overly confident, and I felt as if he was dragging me around the room. Not a trait I admired in a man, reminding me of the late Major Albert Coltrane, a man I had once been betrothed to who came to a sticky end, covered in pea and ham soup. Then, in a split second, the muscle memory returned. My feet moved and I swished my hips as we passed the band.

"You are good, very good, ma chérie," Michel said, dealing me a waft of stale tobacco.

As the dance progressed, memories of Leonard rushed in, as if I was dancing with him, allowing the rhythm and music to guide me. As the dance reached its climax, I met Michel's gaze and I returned it with a hard stare, hoping it delivered the message that I was not to be drawn in by his seduction. I somehow shifted our roles from the start of the dance. I was now the bold and assertive dancer. I noticed a flicker of surprise in his eyes as if it fuelled competition between us. I forgot myself for a few bars. The room around me blurred, as I imagined I was with Leo again. My darling Leo. And then it was over.

I glanced over at the Simpson sisters, the Major, Lottie and Sebastian who were all clapping. I took in a deep breath, feeling somewhat self conscious.

"You are a passionate dancer," Michel said.

"Merci, I danced the tango many times with my late husband."

"Please, I buy you a drink."

"No need, but thank you." I moved away but he clutched onto my hand.

I looked over to our table and the Major was struggling to stand. Sebastian spoke to him and I turned back as Michel led me away.

Sebastian was over in a flash. "May I have the next dance, *Lady* Ellen?" he said, emphasising my title.

"Of course, *Lord* Garthorn," I said and took his hand.

Michel released my other, a look of confusion on his face. Perhaps he hadn't realised I was of the upper classes. "It was my pleasure."

I turned away. "Actually, Sebastian. I feel as if I could do with a drink." Once we were away from Michel, I relaxed a little. "Thank you for cutting in."

"You're a stunning dancer, Ellen," he said. "Michel probably wanted to monopolise you for the remainder of the evening."

"Enchanting!" Major Fitzwilliam said with a smile as we reached the table.

"I reckon he wants you to replace Pearl," Lottie said with a giggle.

"I'm a little embarrassed." I sat in my chair. "I felt as if I was young and carefree again."

"You're still so young," Betty said with a distant smile. "So very young."

A stout man with a bald head approached. "Could I please have this dance?"

"I'm afraid I'm soon to retire, but thank you for asking," I said.

"Ellen, they'll all be asking you to dance now!" Lottie said, wide-eyed, as the man sloped away.

"You were mesmerising," Betty said.

"I have to agree, extremely skilled," Nelly added.

"Michel was a little forceful in my opinion," I said. "I wanted to be a match for him. It's my competitive streak. I let it get the better of me."

"I bet he wasn't expecting that!" Betty said with a chuckle.

"I've seen him with a few ladies," Nelly said with a sniff. "Throwing them around like dolls in the tango."

"I wish I could dance that way." Lottie gazed over to Michel as he approached Pearl, the female host who had changed into a white dress.

"We could have taken lessons here at the hotel," Sebastian said. "It's a shame I have to return to London tomorrow."

A waiter approached, he was around twenty with blond, slicked back hair and a slim frame. "Would you like to order more drinks?" he asked us in a London accent.

"Orange juice for us please, Eddie," Betty said beaming.

"If you could add just a dash of gin to them," Nelly said.

"A couple of dashes," Betty added.

I smiled at the pair with amusement. They were making my stay a little more pleasurable.

"Such a nice young man," Betty said as I turned to the sound of raised voices.

"Return home this instant." A tall man with a receding hairline gestured at a beautiful woman, who wore a daring blue dress which showed off her shoulders with thin straps. It was only just skirting her knees, and was a little too risqué for me. It had a split that showed one of her long legs, and even a flash of thigh when she moved.

"That's the man who owns the pier," Betty said in a loud whisper. "Richard Sheringham, and he's talking to his wife, Violet. They've been married for less than a year."

Betty was indeed a good source of gossip, and I realised that may have been one of the reasons I liked her so much. I took in the scowling man. Richard Sheringham was clean-shaven and appeared to be much older than his wife who was striking. Absolutely beautiful. Her dark hair, almost black, framed her heart-shaped face. Her bright blue eyes stood out against her pale skin, I felt rather mediocre in comparison.

"Go home, Richard, you're embarrassing me." Violet sashayed towards Michel who turned, smiled and then jerked his chin upwards at Mr Sheringham as if waiting for a confrontation.

"Scandalous," the Major said, flanked by the Simpson sisters. Betty's mouth was agape and Nelly's was in a straight line.

"You're embarrassing yourself," Richard Sheringham shouted as Violet took Michel's hand and led him to the dance floor. She swayed a little before getting into hold and their torsos met for a foxtrot.

"I think she's looking for attention," Lottie said as the music began.

"It appears to be working, everyone's watching," Sebastian said as Richard Sheringham stormed out of the room.

"I guess he doesn't want any confrontation, the poor man," Nelly said, then pursed her lips as she watched him leave.

"Your drinks?" Eddie said as he placed them on the table. I noticed him look up as Michel danced by with the now giggling Violet Sheringham.

"Well, I never," Betty said, adjusting her glasses. "I think she's drunk."

"He's playing with fire." Eddie shook his head as he deposited the drinks on the table then returned to the bar.

As we drank, the Major updated us on the progress of England's cricket team, informing us that they had played a test series against South Africa with a comfortable win over three matches. Their first win since 1921. He was interrupted as a heavy and scruffy man stumbled past our table. He was clearly inebriated, with a flushed face and a loose tie. I watched as he made his way across the dance floor, wondering whether he would trip, until he reached Michel Blanc.

He tapped him on the back as the couple slowed at a section of floor not far from our table. "I'm cutting in," he slurred.

"No, you will not, Monsieur Lightfoot," Michel said in his strong French accent. "You will have to wait your turn." He swiftly whisked Violet away and swept her across the dance floor as she laughed, throwing her head back as Michel kissed her neck.

"I say," Sebastian said. "That's really not on!"

"You'll regret you ever came to this town," Mr Lightfoot called out, droplets of saliva caught by the light, as he waved a fist at him. He staggered away, swearing in the most ungentlemanly manner as he passed our table.

"Inexcusable," the Major said, his grey and over-grown brows knitting together.

"Poor old Herbert," Betty said. "He's had a rough time. Eddie told us he used to give lessons here before Michel turned up in Branden Bay and took his job away, about five months back."

"You can't blame Angus Scott," Nelly said, referring to the hotel owner. "Michel's a superior dancer and has more appeal as a host than Mr Lightfoot." She shot a look over at the man who was now at the bar. Eddie filled his glass with whisky before Lightfoot downed it in one go.

"Inebriate!" the Major said as he nursed his brandy.

"He's brought it on himself," Nelly said. "If it wasn't Michel, someone else would have taken his job."

"But he didn't just lose his job, he had to move out too," Betty said. "One minute he's living in The Grand Hotel, and the next he's got no job and living in a pokey room above an undertaker."

"You two know everything that goes on here," Lottie said with her eyes wide open.

Betty continued: "And I've heard he got kicked out of that place and moved above The Branden Arms two weeks ago."

"Not the best place for someone prone to drinking too much alcohol," Nelly added.

"And he lost his host job at the tea dance on the pier," Betty said. "No doubt due to his drinking."

"Or his obsession with Violet," Nelly added.

I turned my gaze to the dance floor when the music concluded. Michel and Violet were static. He clutched her hands in his, talking to her intently. She snatched her hands away took a step backwards, and then hit him straight across the face with the palm of her hand. He stared at her, not even rubbing his cheek, even though it must have stung – we'd heard the sound of the slap from our table.

"And we wanted to go to a jazz club. It's certainly more entertaining in here than I thought it would be," Sebastian said with a laugh as we watched the pair.

Violet stormed across the dance floor and Lottie sat transfixed, her mouth wide open as she gawped at her.

"Hopefully she's returning to her marital home," Nelly said with a sniff before pursing her lips.

We watched Michel go to the opposite end of the bar to where Mr Lightfoot was sitting. He gestured at Eddie the barman, presumably ordering a drink. Eddie pulled a glass down and poured from the same bottle of whisky that he had served Mr Lightfoot from. He grinned at Michel as he spoke to him, then in a flash,

Michel grabbed the young man by the scruff of the neck, nearly pulling him across the bar.

"Did you see that?" Lottie asked me.

"I certainly did." I picked up my drink and took a sip whilst watching the pair.

Michel released Eddie, who adjusted his tie and walked away to serve another customer. I considered whether I should report the matter to the hotel owner, Angus Scott, then returned my gaze to the dance floor and stifled a yawn. As intriguing as the gossip and theatrics were, I really needed to retire.

"I think the evening has drawn to a close for me," I said, having finished the dregs of my brandy. I also wished to check on my dog and relieve the maid I'd asked to watch him for me.

Sebastian stood up and offered me his arm. "I will escort you both to your suite." Since arriving at The Grand Hotel a week before, I'd been keeping a keen eye on Lottie and the young man she was in love with. I'd felt more like a chaperone to the pair, than someone enjoying my own holiday. I was glad that Sebastian was leaving the following morning to return to his parents, the Marquis and Marchioness of Bandberry, at their London residence. It would give me a chance to relax a little. We wished the Simpson sisters and the Major goodnight.

CHAPTER 2

On Monday morning, I rose from bed and gazed at the view of the promenade from my bedroom window. I smiled, recalling the relaxing Sunday Lottie and I had enjoyed together. As much as I missed Hamilton, it had been most pleasant to spend time alone with Lottie, especially with Sebastian away in London. It was a taste of the holiday I'd longed for. The day I'd dreamed of having in Branden Bay, stretching out endlessly, as I relaxed and enjoyed the surroundings. Lottie and I had strolled along the beach as my dog, Prince, bounded over the sands ahead of us. We'd taken a leisurely lunch at the hotel and had retired after enjoying high tea in our suite. I wanted the last days of my extended holiday from Ashcombe to be just as special.

I adored The Grand Hotel and whilst it was not as modern as the new Millar's Hotel where I had begun my trip away from Ashcombe Hall, it held special memories as I'd stayed there with my dear papa when I was a child. Whilst Branden Bay was not far from Ashcombe in miles, staying over in the town had always been a treat, and back in those days it had been more of a relaxed place, where people visited for rest and recuperation. Whilst the pier and fairground had been there, the town didn't have the modern nightlife then that it did now in 1924, with jazz bars and multiple shows, in addition to those at the musical hall and the staid tea dances on the pier. I thoroughly enjoyed the night life as an adult, and intended to increase my social activity, knowing I would soon be returning to the hall and my old life. A part of me wanted to clutch onto the newfound Ellen before I resumed my life as *Lady* Ellen and the responsibilities which came with being custodian of Ashcombe Hall. I wondered how much of my new self I would be able to take back home with me.

I pulled on my dressing gown and entered the main living area of the suite to find Lottie and Prince both awake. Lottie still wore her nightdress and sat in the bay window reading *Debrett's Etiquette & Modern Manners*. She was determined to learn how to become a lady.

She smiled up at me and then placed the book beside her. "Morning, Ellen."

"Did you sleep well?" I asked as she turned her gaze to the promenade as if looking out for someone.

Prince padded over to me and gave me a morning bark.

I stroked my dog's head. "Is Sebastian due back already?" I asked, wondering whether Lottie had received a message from him.

"He said he'd be a couple of days or so," she said. "But he might surprise me." She turned to me. "I feel better looking out for him after what happened, I feel my nerves on edge when he's not here."

"I can imagine," I said. Sebastian had been on a trip with his parents to Ireland to meet a young woman whom they wished him to wed. After they'd announced his engagement without even consulting him, he'd run away in the dead of night, travelling back alone to be reunited with Lottie. Whilst the pair were clearly in love, Sebastian was heir to the estate and title of Bandberry, and Lottie had been brought up in his parents' household amongst the serving staff.

"I doubt he'll arrive yet even if he was travelling today," I said as I stroked Prince's head. "It would be good to sightsee with Sebastian." The young man had such an interest in history. His questions and thirst for knowledge always intensified the enjoyment of our visits. "Hopefully this time we can stick to tourist activities, rather than hunting criminals," I said.

"I hope Ernest comes back, too," she said, using Hamilton's Christian name. She looked at me thoughtfully and I presumed she was deciding whether to broach the subject of myself and Hamilton.

"It's been nice getting to know you, and Sebastian and Ernest," I said. "But we return to the hall soon."

"But Ernest can visit," Lottie said.

"He'll be busy, considering his trip abroad."

"But when he gets back do you think you and he...?" She trailed off.

"I've been quite a different person since I've been away. Ernest may not like me so much once I return to the hall."

"Nonsense. He loves you!"

I laughed. "I think you're getting a little carried away and you may not like me either once we return."

Lottie stood up and took the few short steps between us. "I could never dislike you, Ellen. You've saved my life." She hugged me and I immediately felt overcome. I'd been constantly pushing away my thoughts of Hamilton and the fact that I may not see him before he left for Cairo. Lottie, so open with her feelings, warmed my heart. But I didn't want to allow myself to descend into a mess of emotions.

Prince barked and jumped up at us.

Lottie released me with a laugh. "Are you jealous?" She stroked Prince's soft red hair. He was an Irish setter that I'd rescued as a puppy. He'd been the runt of the litter but had grown into a healthy and strong dog, if a little different lookswise, with short legs for a setter and wonky eyes. He was the most faithful pet anyone could wish for.

"I'll get dressed and take him for a walk," Lottie said. "So we can leave him and go down for our breakfast."

Once Lottie had taken Prince for a quick run, I looked at her supply of paper and envelopes. I had an address which Hamilton was using in London. In that moment, I felt compelled to write to him and explain how I felt. I took a sheet of paper and sat at the small writing desk in the suite. *Shall I really do this?* I asked myself. Part of me realised a relationship between us was unlikely, considering our differences in social standing. Whilst I felt the attraction was mutual, I was the daughter of the late Earl of Ashcombe and Hamilton the son of an accountant. Although my husband Leonard had not held his own title, he was still a member of the upper classes and had lived as such. Whereas Hamilton was extremely middle class with middle class morals. I could not imagine him crossing the social line. Maybe him leaving the country was indeed a good idea, especially when I had so much to consider with the hall. My staff were ageing, and I had to decide the future of the entire estate. But still, the urge to express my feelings spurred me on.

Dear Ernest. I paused over the paper. *I have grown most fond of you over recent months.* I looked at the page and hesitated, considering whether I should tear the letter up. But I continued. *It fills me with sadness to feel that I will no longer see you, enjoy our discussions, walks and shared laughter.* I blushed. *I know that it concerns you that we are from different social positions, however that is meaningless to me. I hope that you will write to me and tell me of your adventures as you hold a special place in my heart. There is no other man I would rather spend my days with.* I looked out of the window, remembering our many walks along the promenade during the day and evenings. I glanced back down at the page. *I will await your return and hope we can spend many more moments together.* I wondered if it was clear that I intended to wait for him and would show no interest in any other man. *With all my love, Ellen.* I hoped that by signing in such a way, he would realise. I wrote his name and the London address on the front of an envelope and affixed a stamp. I was not completely sure I would send it, but still, I popped it into my bag at the moment Lottie breezed in.

"I picked up a fresh bone for Prince." She unwrapped the bone and gave him the treat. "I'll just wash my hands."

As WE DESCENDED the sweeping carpeted staircase, I appreciated that The Grand was indeed grand, with red and golden décor. We entered the main reception and headed towards the smells and sounds of the restaurant where breakfast was being served. The room had high ceilings as it had been built during the Victorian reign and the staff were impeccably turned out in white shirts and red waistcoats. Although there was a mix of all ages amongst the guests, the owner Angus Scott had explained to me that he favoured the more mature resident, as the youngsters were some-what boisterous. Especially those who considered themselves the Bright Young Things.

"Lady Ellen," the maître d' said as we reached the door. "Come this way." He showed us to a table for breakfast, by the window.

Lottie sat down eagerly and looked out to the promenade.

I laughed. "Will you look for Sebastian until the very moment he returns?"

"I can't help it," she said. "I thought I'd lost him and now it makes me nervous if he's not by my side. And I'm looking for the postman."

"Sebastian will be off to university soon," I said as I placed the napkin on my lap.

"I know, it will kill me," she said.

"Don't worry, we'll be so busy when we return to Ashcombe, you'll have enough to take your mind off him."

"He says he'll come to see me as often as he can."

"And we can visit him. I love Oxford."

Lottie turned back and squealed. "Ernest."

I turned in the direction she was looking and my heartbeat quickened as I saw Hamilton seated at a table for one with his newspaper in his hand and a broad smile upon his face. I relaxed as a warmth washed over me, releasing I'd been carrying a tension around with me for days.

Lottie beckoned him over.

"It's wonderful to see you back!" My smile turned into a wide grin as he reached us.

"I left a message for you at the reception," he said. "I returned late last night."

"We haven't picked our messages up yet," Lottie said. "There might be one from Sebastian." She stood up.

"After our breakfast, we will check," I said and she returned to her chair as a waitress delivered a pot of coffee to our table.

"Please, join us," I said to Hamilton.

Once a place had been set for Hamilton at our table, the waitress requested our order. "What would you like to eat, my lady?"

"Could I please have the cooked breakfast with my eggs scrambled?"

"Of course, and Miss Penny?"

"I'll have the same," Lottie said.

"And Captain Hamilton?"

"Same for me as well, thank you."

I was looking forward to my food and noticed that as soon as I'd seen Hamilton, my appetite had returned with much gusto.

"We've been talking about what sightseeing we'd like to do," Lottie said to Hamilton. "And how nice it would be if you'd come back and Sebastian too and we can all go sightseeing together."

Hamilton glanced at me as if waiting for my permission.

"It would be super if you could join us. What are your commitments?" I asked him.

"I must visit London again this week to sign papers. And then the final details of the exact sail date from Plymouth will be confirmed. But it will not be for at least one week, as the ship has yet to return from its current sailing." He smiled at me. "I would love to join your sightseeing trips. What activities have you in mind?"

"I'd quite like to take a drive through the countryside with a picnic," I said. "And to simply relax on the beach in a deck chair."

"I'd love to take a swim," Lottie added.

"That sounds fun," I said. "If the weather remains pleasant. And we'll need to purchase swimsuits."

"I'd love to take to the water," Hamilton said.

I sipped my coffee, wondering whether it would be improper to splash about in the waves with Hamilton. I sat back smiling. At last, my peaceful holiday had begun.

A piercing scream shattered the calm.

Lottie spun around. "What was that?"

I placed my hand upon hers. "Nothing we need to concern ourselves with."

"But someone screamed!" she said.

"I'm sure it's nothing," Hamilton said, but he keenly watched the door of the restaurant with his eyebrows raised.

"It was pretty loud," Lottie said slowly as she also trained her eyes on the door.

I turned and focussed on the view from the window, telling myself the scream was nothing to cause alarm. *Maybe a guest spotted a spider?* I told myself.

The rest of those taking breakfast had fallen silent, and I heard the door of the restaurant open and footsteps tap upon the wooden floors behind me. I resisted the temptation to turn around.

"It's Angus Scott," Hamilton said in a low voice. "He's heading this way." He sat to attention in his seat as the footsteps became louder. "He looks jolly fearful."

"His face is deep red," Lottie whispered.

The hotel owner stopped as he reached our table. "Lady Ellen."

I reluctantly turned around and my heart sank as I saw his expression. His face was indeed flushed. Looking into his eyes, I knew that what he had to say was something I did not want to hear.

"Is there something the matter, Mr Scott?" I asked, dreading the answer.

"There's a body in the ballroom!"

CHAPTER 3

"Have you called the police?" I asked Angus Scott.

"The Sergeant is on his way, and the doctor has been called."

"I'm certain Sergeant Chambers will handle the matter efficiently," I said, determined to avoid any involvement.

"Do you know what happened?" Hamilton asked.

"Who's a goner?" Lottie added.

I noticed that Lottie's elocution slipped considerably when excited.

"It's a man, that's all I know," Angus said. "The maid who found him is hysterical. The maître d' is attempting to calm her down. I need to go to the ballroom now, but I was wondering if you wanted to assist, with your expertise in such matters." He looked me directly in the eye.

"I'm no expert, Mr Scott," I said. "I've simply found

myself in the wrong place at the wrong time and I've no appetite for gazing upon the dead." Although I was used to seeing the dead, following my stint as a nurse during and after the war at my convalescent home, where I sadly lost a few men, it was an experience one could never get used to.

"Do you suspect foul play?" Hamilton asked as I noticed that guests at nearby tables were staring our way.

"I've no idea of the facts," Angus said in a quiet voice, running a hand through his red hair. I realised he was likely delaying his own entry into the ballroom, not wishing to witness the scene. And I did not blame the fellow.

I lowered my voice too, as the other guests gawped at us. "Why don't you take a seat and wait until the police arrive. It's not for everyone's stomach."

He pulled a chair from a nearby table and sat down with us.

"Take a couple of deep breaths, Angus," I said, fearing the man was close to passing out. His lips had paled in colour and I instinctively poured him a glass of water from the jug on the table and handed it to him.

"What if it's someone I know?" he whispered, then drank the glass of water.

"I think you need to calm down, Mr Scott," Hamilton said gently.

"It could simply be an elderly customer with a heart condition," I added in what I hoped was a soothing voice. I wasn't sure I'd entirely managed to hide the tremble.

"Exactly, it could be entirely natural causes," Hamilton added. "However, if you'd like to investigate, I'll accompany you."

Angus groaned. "Dora's due home in less than two weeks. I don't want her retuning to find someone has been murdered at the hotel! I need the place calm and quiet, considering her nerves. I want to integrate her back into the hotel, so we can spend our days together here, rather than her cooped up in our house, alone. How is she going to feel with a dead body turning up in our ballroom?"

I had helped Angus with his troubled wife, and found Dora a place with an eminent psychologist I had previously appointed to attend to the men who were in my care at Ashcombe Hall. It was not only physical ailments the soldiers suffered from – indeed, Hamilton had also suffered from what they called 'shell shock' when he had rested at Ashcombe.

"Let's leave it to the police," I said. "I'm sure there's a reasonable explanation for the fellow's demise."

The maître d' approached Angus, his expression tense. "Mr Scott, the doctor's here."

Angus sighed and asked us to excuse him, and then left the room as our breakfasts were delivered by a flustered pair of waitresses. As I looked down at my food, I found that my appetite was again suppressed.

"I wonder what someone was doing in the ballroom

on their own?" Lottie said, tucking into her food as if she was starving.

"It must have happened after the ballroom was closed," Hamilton said. "Otherwise, someone would have witnessed the poor fellow's death."

"It's not open on a Sunday evening," I said.

"But remember, Michel gives private lessons on a Sunday, don't he," Lottie said.

"Doesn't he," I said, correcting her diction.

"Doesn't he," she repeated in a quiet voice.

"What time do the dance lessons finish?" Hamilton asked her.

I cut in. "We don't want to know. We're all in need of a relaxing period before we are parted." I paused as Hamilton gazed into my eyes and I felt he acknowledged my reference to us having limited time together. I tore my gaze away and glanced at Lottie. "I wish not to become involved."

Lottie began to wolf down her food, clearly ignoring my statement and eager to discover exactly what was afoot.

"Charlotte Anne Penny," I said, using her full name to emphasise my point. "Consider your manners."

"Oh, yes, sorry," she said, then looked at Hamilton who I was convinced winked at her. She sat up straight but continued to eat with a measure of speed.

A waitress approached the table. She was wringing her hands and biting her lip.

"What's happening?" Hamilton asked her.

I sighed, recognising the spark of curiosity in his

eyes that mirrored Lottie's. They were clearly ignoring my plea to not take an interest. I wanted to cover my ears to prevent myself from hearing.

"A gentleman has been taken ill," she said as she placed a plate of toast and preserves on the table.

"Ill?" Lottie asked. "I thought he was dead!" Her voice was a little loud and the hubbub around us came to a stop.

"Well, the doctor needs to confirm it but, yes," the waitress whispered, then continued. "We've been told not to talk about it until the police have been in."

Whispers began to float around the restaurant like ripples from a stone thrown into a pond, and the waitress looked about nervously as if expecting a reprimand.

"Who is he?" Lottie asked. "Or should I say was?"

"I'm not permitted to say," the waitress said as her bottom lip trembled. "Would you like a refill of coffee? We're closing breakfast early."

"No, thank you," I replied in a soothing voice, then shot a sideways glance at Hamilton and then Lottie as the waitress hurried away.

Hamilton leaned forward and spoke in a low voice. "I'm back in town and this happens? I'm beginning to feel like a bad penny, bringing bad luck with me."

"I can sympathise with that," I said with a sigh. "But at present there's no mention of foul play. And even if there were, surely you would like some time to relax before you travel to Cairo?"

"Ah," Hamilton said as a small smile spread across his face. "You're sensing my intrigue."

I put my head on one side. "I've enjoyed our adventures together, but it's essential that I return to the hall refreshed." I placed my cutlery together on the plate, having hardly touched my food, and glanced out of the window, pretending there had been no mention of a body. Many who came to Branden Bay indulged in a little too much excitement and many of the clientele were elderly. No doubt a poor man had collapsed, maybe after a little too much wine, in a dark corner of the ballroom and was not discovered until the morning. Although as I calmed myself, a dread continued to seep into my veins as a voice in my head told me otherwise, and that I was again to be sucked into a drama. And from the expressions on Lottie and Hamilton's faces, I would have a battle on my hands to drag them away from it.

Angus soon returned with his eyes wide, and I could tell before he reached us that the death in question was far from a case of natural causes.

He sat down. "It's murder," he whispered, his voice trembling. "The doctor confirmed he was strangled."

"It's terrible, but we must leave it to the police," I said quietly.

Lottie put her hand to her neck. "Does this mean there's a strangler on the loose?"

The couple at the next table stared at us.

Angus looked about him and realised he would have to say something. He rose from his chair and addressed the room. "Unfortunately, there has been an incident in the ballroom. The police will be interviewing all hotel guests shortly." Chatter began and Angus put his hand up as if to ask for silence. When the room hushed he spoke again: "There is no cause for alarm." He turned back to us as those present hurriedly prepared to leave the room. He sat down. "Please, can you help?" he asked me.

"Angus, I'm not what you need. Leave this to the police," I said. I especially wanted to leave it to the police if Scotland Yard were to be involved. There was an inspector that I was far from fond of. In that moment, I wished I'd chosen a different town for my last two weeks of rest. Somewhere sedate – or simply to have remained with my friend whom I had recently visited, Lady Phoebe Denham, of Denham Hall.

I stood up. "Angus, if you would care to excuse us, we've left my dog alone long enough, we don't want him to ruin your furnishings." I softened my voice. "I'm sure the police will deal with this matter for you." I looked to Lottie and then to Hamilton, who were still seated and making no effort to stand. "Lottie, Ernest? It's the ideal weather for a walk along the beach." I knew neither would refuse me and it would remove us from the hotel and away from the commotion.

"Before we go," Hamilton said to Angus as he rose from his chair. "Who was the unfortunate man?"

Angus sighed. "It was a much-valued member of staff."

"How awful," I said, having assumed it had been a guest.

The door swung open and Sergeant Chambers entered and gave me a stern stare as he approached us.

"To clarify, Sergeant," I said before he could speak. "I have expressed to Mr Scott that I'm sure you will have the investigation completely under control."

"That's right, my lady. And as helpful as you've been, this is a huge operation, with a hotel full of people."

"We will leave it in your capable hands," I said.

Chambers appeared relieved. "If you could provide us with details of the French dancer's next of kin." Chambers pulled out his notebook and looked expectantly at the hotel owner.

The dead man is Michel Blanc? I thought and gulped, having danced with the fellow so publicly two evenings before. Even though he was far from a charming man, I still felt sorry for the fellow. I had judged that he was only a few years older than myself.

"We have no such details," Angus replied. "It's the first thing I did when I discovered the identity of the victim. Michel's file is empty of personal details. Only records of the payments we have made to him and his contract of employment."

"And where's Pearl, the female host?" Lottie asked, jumping in before Chambers could speak.

"She left town for America," Angus said. "But that was Sunday morning when Michel was very much alive. I took her to the station myself and helped her onto the train."

"Where in France did Michel live?" Hamilton asked.

Chambers raised his eyebrows as he looked at me, Hamilton and then to Lottie, who blushed and lowered her eyes.

"Sorry, we didn't mean to interfere," I said in an airy voice, realising I was already finding myself being drawn in and knew the best course of action was for me to extract Lottie, Hamilton and myself from the conversation.

"I'm not sure exactly," Angus said to Hamilton, not at all put off by our involvement. "I will check with the receptionist."

"We'll leave you to your investigations," I said to Chambers, then raised my eyebrows at Lottie. "Come along, Lottie." I turned to Ernest who was just as interested. "Captain Hamilton?"

"Of course, yes," Hamilton said. "Good luck with your inquiries, Sergeant."

"Lottie," I whispered. "Come along." She lagged behind, no doubt straining to hear the continuing conversation.

Hamilton closed the door behind us as we left the restaurant.

"Lady Ellen."

I spotted Betty waving at me. She was sitting at a table just inside the cards room with Nelly and Major Fitzwilliam. I turned to Hamilton. "We've become acquainted with a few hotel guests whilst staying here.

35

I'll introduce you to them and then I'm keen for some fresh air. Lottie, could you collect Prince for me?" I opened my bag and immediately saw the letter I'd written earlier that morning to Hamilton and blushed, pushing it to the side so that I could locate the suite key. Once extracted, I handed it to her.

Hamilton and I approached the cards room. Its heavy oak door was wedged open, no doubt to air the room during the day, for it became extremely smoke-filled in the evenings. The scent of the Major's cigar greeted us. Gambling was not permitted, but it was clear that money certainly changed hands between those playing. The tables were draped in red velvet in the hotel's signature shade, and Nelly collected the cards and shuffled them before placing them neatly in front of her and then looked up as we approached. Betty beckoned me to take a seat beside her and I realised that this brief introduction was likely to be none of the sort. It was clear the subject she wished to discuss. All three pairs of eyes fell upon me as if expecting a full debrief.

"This is Captain Ernest Hamilton," I said as I gestured at him, not mentioning the death at all. "And this is Miss Betty Simpson and Miss Nelly Simpson, who are sisters."

Betty put a hand to her chest. "We've heard all about you. And you are indeed a dashing man."

Hamilton raised an eyebrow at me, a hint of a question in his eyes.

"Lottie described you well," Nelly quickly added, maybe realising what her sister had implied.

"Oh, yes. I'm most flattered," he stuttered.

"And this is Major Walter Fitzwilliam," I said.

"Pleasure," the Major said with a nod.

"Pleased to meet you all," Hamilton said.

"So," Betty said, lowering her voice, "who strangled Michel Blanc? We heard the staff discussing it."

Nelly shook her head, her mouth in a straight line. "He was so young."

"Thirty-two," the Major added.

Betty turned to me. "Is that why you were staying here? Did he know his life was in danger and you were brought in to protect him? Is that why you danced with him so closely Saturday night?"

I was rather stunned and turned to see Hamilton glancing at me with a frown.

"And now it's happened," Betty said. "He's been killed while you were protecting him?"

It was then that the penny dropped. I'd been convinced that Betty and Nelly were in awe of me due to my title; the fact that I was of the upper classes, a lady with an entire estate. But it was clear in that moment that the fascination was entirely due to my local reputation for solving crime. I paused and took in their eager expressions. As they'd not mentioned my sleuthing before, I'd assumed they were unaware of my history. That was silly of me. They'd been staying in Branden Bay for weeks, and realising their thirst for gossip, I should have expected them to be au fait with my previous investigations, considering nothing appeared to escape their attention.

"Will you..." the Major lowered his voice to a whisper "...catch the blighter?"

"Absolutely not," I said a little too loudly. "I'm simply here for rest and recuperation before returning to Ashcombe Hall."

Luckily at that point, Lottie appeared with Prince. "He's desperate to go outside, Ellen," she said from the doorway, not wanting him to walk on the plush carpets of the cards room. She stroked his head. "Calm down, boy."

"We must leave now," I said to the trio.

"We'll see you at dinner, though?" Betty asked excitedly as Nelly began to deal their next round of cards.

I was sure I heard Hamilton sigh as we left the room.

CHAPTER 4

Outside in the pleasant September sunshine, I breathed a sigh of relief as the tension ebbed away. Hamilton walked alongside me as Lottie was pulled along before us by Prince tugging on his leash. My dog became excited as we crossed the road to the promenade, dragging Lottie towards the sands. The wind tousled her bobbed hair. I smiled and pushed my own hair from my eyes as it was blown by a strong gust. It was good to be outside without a hat. I'd never venture to the village in Ashcombe without my head covered, but here in Branden Bay I'd done so a few times. Indeed, I'd partaken in other activities which I would not do at home. Such as walking arm in arm with a gentleman, as I was with Hamilton.

"It's really windy, I'll take Prince on the sand," Lottie called out to us. "You two stay up here if you like. In the shelter."

Hamilton and myself approached the Victorian

style shelter made from iron with glass windows which protected us from the strong winds. The sea was charging in with huge white crested waves.

"The tide will be turning soon," Hamilton said checking his watch. "Once it's on its way out, the wind will calm down." He sat beside me. "So, I take it you knew the dead man? You danced with him?"

"I was not acquainted with him as such, he was the dance host and I tangoed with him on Saturday evening. To be honest, I did not warm to the fellow. He was somewhat forceful, and Sebastian had to cut in to rescue me from his clutches."

"Really?" Hamilton glared.

I gave a short laugh. "Sorry, that sounded a lot more dramatic than it was. It was simply that the fellow had hold of my hand and would not let go. If I were to investigate, which I'm not going to, there would be quite a few suspects. It was clear from the evening I spent watching him, that he was an unpopular man."

"And the fellow was French?"

"Indeed. He had an extremely strong accent. He was sure of himself and clearly not afraid to upset other people, as he had more than one confrontation whilst we were there."

"Ellen, you already have a suspect list in your head, don't you?" Hamilton gave me a sideways grin.

I found it difficult not to smile back. "Everyone who was at the dance on Saturday night will have a suspect list. He's a man that clearly enjoyed wooing women and…" I already felt myself being sucked in. "I'm sure Chambers will take the lead."

"Ellen, you must be curious. Do you have any idea who committed this abhorrent crime?"

I turned and glanced at Hamilton and felt warm in the shelter. We'd become so close. How would I feel when he sailed away for Cairo? I held my bag, thinking of the letter inside, revealing between the lines that I felt love for him.

"I can see it in your eyes," he said. "You're hiding something, and I know what it is."

"You do?" I gulped, waiting for him to say that he knew I cared deeply for him.

"You wish to investigate."

I relaxed then turned away, focussing my eyes on the sands. "No, honestly I don't." I could not help a small smile. "I realise that you're trying to encourage me, but let's leave this one to the police. I would like to enjoy the little time we have left to spend together." I stopped, realising I'd said too much. I ran a hand over my hair. "But I expect to be questioned, since I danced with the fellow."

"What will you say?"

"That he was a little forceful with his flirtation. He did not take no for an answer. I could have dealt with the situation myself, but it would indeed have been an embarrassing spectacle and now the man is dead, it's a relief there was no visible confrontation between us." I watched Lottie throw a stick for Prince. I gestured in her direction. "The tide has turned, let's join Lottie on the sands."

We reached Lottie who was waiting for us. Part of me hoped Hamilton's contract for the trip to Cairo would fall through so that he could remain in England with us. We walked along the beach and I decided to push all thoughts of the hall, of romance and of the strangled Michel Blanc from my mind. The sun was already warm mixed with the variable temperature of occasional gusts of wind – some warm and some with a chill. I strode along the beach, watching Prince bound up and down with sticks for Hamilton to throw for him. I loved to see my dog free and running. He'd been used to six years of freedom on the estate and had spent much of the previous months cooped up inside. After a shaky start where he was tearing up cushions, he'd settled down and was better behaved, but he was really only himself when experiencing the outside world which he clearly loved.

We walked the length of the beach and stopped at the end where there was a small jetty. Lottie sat on it looking out to the estuary, and I walked towards the rocky face at the end of the beach, looking up to Millar's Hotel perched at the top. Modern and built in white, it resembled an angel overseeing the bay. I spotted the balcony of the suite I had stayed in when I'd started my extended break from the hall. I felt as if I had been away forever, so much had transpired. The hotel was undergoing renovations as the new custodians were adding a spa to relaunch it. I felt a little uneasy as I was now in residence of a second hotel where death had occurred.

Hamilton and I sat on a large rock as Prince ran in circles then lolloped onto the sand before me, panting with his pink tongue hanging out. After a ten minute rest, I called to Lottie and beckoned her.

"Prince needs water," I said. "Let's make our return along Beach Road and find somewhere he can refresh himself." I quite fancied a refreshment myself, and a quiet cup of tea was unlikely at The Grand that day.

We headed up the beach to the promenade.

"It's a lot to expect you to come and go to London like this," I said to Hamilton.

"It was me that decided to break my London visit and return here," he said. "No fault of the client. I was keen to… I wanted to…" He trailed off.

I stared back at him and I remembered again the letter in my bag. I smiled to myself, knowing that he had inconvenienced himself because he wished to spend more time with me.

"I'm pleased we'll spend some time together before I go. And with Lottie of course," he added quickly and turned away.

"I do hope you'll visit Ashcombe when you return. How long do you expect to be gone?" I asked.

"The current consignment is expected to take at least six weeks — maybe longer."

"So you won't be back until late autumn?" I failed to keep the disappointment from my voice.

Back on the promenade, we stamped the sand from

our shoes before crossing the road. As we did, I noticed a couple I recognised walking down the slope from the hill where Millar's Hotel was situated. It was John Breckon, the hotel's manager and Norma Lloyd, the cook. They were romantically involved.

"Lady Ellen," Norma said as we reached them. "It's so good to see you."

Prince attempted to jump up at her and Lottie pulled him back, having already affixed his leash.

"We're looking for water for Prince," I said.

"Come to Isla's café with us," Norma said. "My friend runs it and she loves dogs."

"That would be nice," I said. It wasn't only Prince that was thirsty; with the sand laden wind, my mouth felt rather dry.

Inside the café, Norma's friend, Isla, placed a large bowl of water on the floor for Prince and then brought two pots of tea and cups for us.

"How are the renovations going up at Millar's?" I asked Mr Breckon. They clearly had not learned yet of the demise of Michel Blanc and that pleased me. I wanted to pretend that the sorry affair had not happened.

"They're making good progress," he said.

"I'm going to miss the orangery," Norma said with a sigh. "It was so beautiful."

"It makes business sense," Mr Breckon said, "to build the spa there, which will keep customers coming in the cooler months. The hotel needs to appear different after what happened to poor Mr Millar."

"It's going to be very exotic," Norma added. "I don't know if we can stay there."

"Why's that?" I asked.

"They're bringing in a new menu and I'm not getting along with the recipes."

The new owners had been living in India. I'd loved the food when I'd visited the country, and I would certainly be looking forward to a meal there once they reopened.

Norma continued: "I've never chopped so many onions in all me days, me eyes are weeping all morning. The hours of preparation will be tough as it's bad enough now, when we're only cooking for the family and workers." She lowered her voice. "And the spices play havoc with my John's stomach."

Mr Breckon's face changed colour to a deep shade of red. "Norma, I'm sure Lady Ellen is not interested."

Hamilton frowned. He clearly found the talk of bodily functions vulgar, however as a trained nurse it did not bother me one bit, and Lottie giggled.

"If we don't leave, I think we'll be given the boot." Norma looked to Breckon and then back at me. "Well, me. I'll get the sack. Polly's getting on really well with it and she's fond of the new chef." She sighed. "I'm just too long in the tooth. And there's no vacancy at The Grand. I already asked Chef Moreau." The French chef at The Grand had once worked at Millar's. It popped into my head that he might have some information about Michel Blanc, considering they were fellow countrymen, then pushed it from my mind.

Don't get involved, I warned myself. I looked to Lottie and gave my head a short shake, not wanting the mention of The Grand to lead to a conversation about murder.

"After everything that's happened," Breckon said. "I have to admit, I'd prefer a new position as well."

"We're both applying for jobs at an hotel in Minehead," Norma said.

"Maybe a new start would be good," Hamilton said.

"Especially with another murder in Branden Bay," Lottie added wistfully.

"Another murder?" Breckon asked, his eyes widening.

I pursed my lips and gave Lottie a rather hard stare.

"Oh, sorry." Lottie bit her lip.

I turned to Norma and Breckon. "We don't know the details yet," I said, realising that it had been naive of me to think we could have a pleasant cup of tea without any mention of the death.

"Well, he didn't strangle himself, did he?" Lottie muttered.

"The French dance host at The Grand was strangled," Hamilton confirmed as if briefing a team. "His body was found this morning in the ballroom." There was a touch of intrigue in his voice.

"Is this true?" Norma asked me, placing her hand to her chest.

"I'm afraid it is," I said.

"Old Flint'll be upset," Norma said. "I heard a whisper she was planning on having lessons with him."

Mrs Flint was the housekeeping manager at Millar's hotel. "Any idea who done it?"

"I've no wish to become involved," I said.

"Some man shouted at him," Lottie said. "When we were there Saturday night. And then this other bloke, who used to be the dancer there, tried to cut in on a dance. He had a face like thunder he did." Lottie took a sip of her tea. "And then, the man's wife slapped Michel around the face." She gave me a guilty glance before delivering her next line. "And when Michel was at the bar, he grabbed the barman and nearly pulled him over the top of it."

"Lottie," I said, realising she was now too excited to silence. "I think you're exaggerating and we must not interfere."

"I can understand your position, my lady, with you wanting a quiet break," Norma said, but her eyes were also now alight.

"Sergeant Chambers has everything under control," I said.

"I understand, completely," Breckon said before raising his eyebrows at Norma, clearly also picking up her intrigue. Mr Breckon appeared to be a man who preferred an ordered life.

"Exactly, Mr Breckon, I'm glad you appreciate my position." I shot a look at both of my companions, and Prince whined from underneath the table.

"But you're good at investigating," Norma said. "You've a nose for it."

"Not this time. Otherwise, I'll be leaving with you

both for Minehead," I said with a short laugh. "When are you attending the interview?" I asked them, wishing for a change of subject.

"Tomorrow," Breckon said.

"We're staying over," Norma said with a smile.

Breckon flushed a little. "We'd better be getting back, Norma, seeing as we're having the next two days off."

"I wish I could just up and leave Millar's right now," she said.

I smiled as they left. They were a most suited couple, and I genuinely wished them well. Their relationship was relatively new and I hoped that one day they would marry. I stood up, dreading our return to The Grand Hotel as it would be impossible to escape discussions concerning the death of Michel Blanc.

CHAPTER 5

$\mathcal{W}$e returned to The Grand Hotel to find a team of police officers already questioning guests.

Angus Scott rushed over as soon as he spotted us. "They're interviewing everyone. Fortunately, they've already taken away poor Michel." He paused as if remembering the sight. "If you could find time to speak to the officers, they're working their way through the guest register."

"Let's do this now," I said to Lottie, wanting to say my piece and then leave them to it.

"I will take Prince," Hamilton said and Lottie passed him the leash.

We approached PC Ryan who had become free.

"My lady, Sergeant Chambers would like a word with you in person – he's speaking to everyone who interacted with Michel Blanc personally."

"I only danced with him briefly," I said.

"He still insists on speaking to you... Oh, he's free now." He nodded over to the sergeant.

"Shall I get paper so I can take notes?" Lottie asked eagerly.

"No," I said firmly.

"Lady Ellen," Chambers said as we approached. "I understand you interacted with the victim. I'd be interested in your observations." He shot a glance to Lottie. "Did you meet Michel Blanc also?"

"I never spoke to him," she said, her eyes alight. "But I saw what he got up to."

"It's tragic that Michel Blanc lost his life," I said as I stared at Lottie.

"Oh, yes, awful," Lottie said, changing her facial expression from excitement to a concerned frown.

"Is it true he was strangled?" Hamilton asked. I hadn't realised he'd also followed us.

"I'm the one asking the questions. Captain, where were you Sunday evening?"

"I arrived yesterday at nine pm, checked in and went straight to my room. I'd travelled in from London."

"There's no need for me to speak to you, then."

Prince whined. I knew he was hungry.

"Could you take Prince to my suite, Ernest?" I asked him. "Whilst Lottie and I speak to the sergeant."

"Of course."

Lottie handed him the key. "He's got a bone up there."

Hamilton sloped off and I felt a half smile form on

my lips knowing he wanted to be involved, and pleased at the same time as I intended to help the police as much as I could without having to hear another word on the matter.

"Miss Penny," Chambers said. "What were your observations?"

"He pranced around like he loved himself," Lottie said. "And Sebastian had to save Ellen when he insisted she dance with him."

"Is Lord Garthorn staying here too?" the Sergeant asked.

"He returned to London, before the man died," I said. "I agree with Lottie – Michel Blanc had an undeniably arrogant air, and on the evening before his demise, there were several people who appeared to dislike him. You might wish to speak with them."

"Such as?" He poised his pencil over his notebook.

"Well, I'm not entirely sure of who they were," I said then looked to my right as the Simpson sisters entered. I lowered my voice. "The women who have just walked in are long term resident guests and know everyone and their business. If I was you, I'd ask them. We were sitting with them and witnessed a few interactions between Michel and other people. I'm not sure of the names of those involved."

"I remember," Lottie said, seemingly reluctant to pass the matter over to Betty and Nelly. "Two of the people were Mr and Mrs Sheringham who own the pier. Mrs Sheringham was dressed up with lots of make-up, and she was dancing with Michel, really close. Her husband shouted at her saying she was making a fool of herself. Then there was the old dance host, he tried to cut in."

"And his name?" Chambers asked.

"Er…"

"Herbert Lightfoot," I added reluctantly.

Lottie continued: "He stormed over to the bar and then not three minutes later, Mrs Sheringham slapped the Frenchman right across the face! Then Michel goes over to the bar a few feet from the other dancer and then took it out on poor Eddie, nearly dragging him over the top."

"Eddie is a barman?" Chambers asked Lottie, apparently deciding that she was a better source of information than myself.

"Yeah, he's from London. Poor fella. Michel pulled him by the scruff of his neck! Didn't hear what was said, but he weren't happy and Eddie just laughed at him."

"This was all Saturday evening," I said. "We did not set eyes upon Michel at all yesterday."

"So how did you interact with the victim? My lady?" he asked me directly.

"As Lottie said, I danced with him, as did many ladies that evening. He asked me for another dance, I declined, yet he did not release my hand so Lord Garthorn stepped in. That was my last interaction with the fellow."

"Thank you for this information. I'm sure Inspector Stone will appreciate it."

"Will he be involved?" I asked.

"I'm afraid so. He's on his way."

"I do hope he doesn't feel the need to speak with me personally."

"My lady, I will do my best to ensure he'll not bother you. And I assume you'll not be taking it upon yourself to investigate this matter?"

"Of course not. I've had more than enough excitement this summer. Good luck with finding the perpetrator," I said. "Come along Lottie, let's leave Sergeant Chambers to his investigation."

As we walked away, Lottie whispered to me. "Are you sure you don't want us to find out who done it?"

"Yes, of course I am," I said. "And I will be most upset if you interfere."

"I understand," Lottie said with a sorrowful tone.

WE KEPT to my suite for the remainder of the day, planning out the next few days ahead and keeping away from the commotion downstairs. I'd noticed police cars arriving and leaving, and wondered whether Inspector Stone was in the building, which too was a reason to keep out of the way. We had ordered luncheon to the suite and I completed a couple of puzzles in my copy of the Strand Magazine. Hamilton read his newspaper and Lottie continued to read her copy of *Debrett's Etiquette and Modern Manners* asking me questions intermittently on what was proper in certain situations. Prince slept by the unlit fireplace. I cherished those quiet moments with Lottie and Hamilton – they felt like home to me. However, we could not hide all day, so Hamilton left at four and we agreed to meet him at the hotel bar at seven o'clock before our evening meal booking of half past.

As we reached the bar, we found Hamilton sitting with the Simpson sisters and between them, as usual, was the Major. Hamilton nodded at Betty with a frozen smile upon his face.

"The police have arrested someone," Betty said before I could even sit down. "A woman."

"Quite a commotion," Nelly added.

"Uproar!" Fitzwilliam said.

A woman? I thought. I was relieved that the matter had been resolved so quickly, but was still a little shocked that a woman had strangled Michel Blanc. *Was it Violet Sheringham?* I thought.

"What happened?" Lottie asked as if she was peeved the case had been solved without our involvement.

"She arrived and asked if anyone had seen her scarf," Nelly said. "We heard it from the cards room."

"And when she described it to the police, well. It must have been the one used to strangle him," Betty said.

"A tall policeman in a suit arrested her on the spot," Nelly added. "They clearly think she did it."

My heart sank a little as I was already unconvinced. "Why would the murderer pop back to collect the murder weapon?"

"Exactly," Nelly said, sitting back in her seat and placing her hands on her lap.

"Nelly thinks they've got the wrong person. Do you?" Betty asked me as she adjusted her glasses.

"It's not my concern," I replied, looking up to try to catch Eddie's eye, as I was in need of a drink.

"Although," Hamilton said. "We surely would not want to sit by and see a miscarriage of justice."

"It wouldn't be fair for a woman to be hanged when she never done it," Lottie added.

"When she didn't do it," I said, correcting her English – not because I was concerned, I was rather fond of her natural London dialect. However, as she had hopes of becoming the next Marchioness of Band-berry, as impossible a goal as that appeared, she'd asked me for help with smartening up her elocution, so I felt obliged to point it out.

"Sorry, didn't do it." Lottie beamed at me and sat up straight in her chair and then spoke in a clear and steady voice. "What are we to do?"

"I'm sure Sergeant Chambers has everything under control," I said. "The man is intelligent."

"I don't have as much faith in Inspector Stone," Hamilton grumbled. "It was probably him who arrested the poor woman." I sensed that he disliked the fellow even more than I did. "The man seems to think the most unlikely people criminals."

"That's true," I said. The Inspector had accused both Hamilton and myself of crimes since we'd been in Branden Bay, even suggesting that Hamilton, an upstanding gentleman who had fought for his country, was a hunted murderer called the Vigilante Slasher.

"Excuse me."

I turned to find the hotel receptionist before me, holding a slip of paper.

"Yes?" I asked.

"A message for you, my lady."

"Thank you," I said, taking it from her and wondering whether it was a message from home, considering my stay in Branden Bay was drawing to a close.

She bobbed an awkward curtsy, then hurried away.

I felt the gaze of those seated with me as I opened the paper and groaned. I read it aloud. "Lady Ellen, Inspector Stone requests that you meet him at Branden Bay police station immediately."

"What on earth does the man want?" Hamilton said in exasperation.

"I reckon he's got a thing for you," Lottie said with a giggle and a measure of excitement that she appeared to be finding hard to contain. "Shall I come too?"

"The fellow has only recently been married, so I doubt that he has any romantic notions as far as I'm concerned," I said in a haughty voice. "It's likely that he holds a grudge against me."

"I concur with that theory," Hamilton said. "You've shown the chap to be the inept man he is. Would you like me to accompany you?"

"Surely you can have your dinner first, my lady?" Nelly said.

"Shall we all go?" Betty asked eagerly.

I imagined Inspector Stone's face if I arrived with an entourage. "It's probably better if I go alone."

"I will escort you and wait for you," Hamilton said.

"Thank you, that would be nice." I did not require an escort, but I very much liked the idea of the walk with Hamilton by my side.

"We'll look after Lottie," Betty said affectionately.

EVEN THOUGH I dreaded meeting the Inspector again, I enjoyed the stroll up the High Street to the police station with Hamilton immensely. As I took his arm, it was lovely to see him free of the stick that he'd been using since he left the convalescent home I'd run at Ashcombe Hall since the war. He'd decided to carry it as a mental crutch until he felt he had overcome his ailments of the head. I wondered if he had totally been cured of his shell shock or whether it had scarred him for life.

As we walked, we reminisced about our time in Branden Bay, recalling our visits the jazz bars, walks along the promenade and the warmth of the summer. By the time we'd reached the police station, I had clean forgotten that I'd been summonsed by the odious Inspector Stone. No doubt he would take every opportunity to put me down. I assumed he had summonsed me to issue a warning that I should not interfere with his work. This did not please me, since I'd been more than helpful to him in the past. I was not in competition with the police, I'd wanted justice to be done and had no appetite for feelings of glory.

I turned and took the steps up to the police station and approached the desk where PC Ryan was on duty.

"Lady Ellen," he said. "Thank you for coming."

"I shall wait for you," Hamilton said as he took a chair in the waiting area.

PC Ryan lowered his voice. "Stone's in a foul mood. I thought I'd warn you."

"I've never seen the fellow cheerful," I said with a small laugh. "So it will be the usual experience for me." I smiled at him. "But thank you for the warning."

PC Ryan left for a short while and Inspector Stone soon appeared in the reception.

"There you are!" he barked at me.

"I came as soon as I received your message," I said, although I really had no reason to justify what he appeared to consider was a late appearance. "And I hope this will not take too long as I have yet to eat," I added, to emphasise that I was not to be bullied by him.

He pointed at me in a vulgar fashion. "I'm telling you right away, get in there and then out as soon as possible. I don't want any of your meddling."

"Inspector Stone." Hamilton rose from his chair. "Have some respect, man!"

"I can assure you," I said to Stone, "I have no wish to be here and am only here at your request."

He gave a sarcastic laugh. "And I can assure you, my *lady*, that you are the last person I would have asked to come to the station." His eye twitched.

"In that case, Inspector, I'll not give you any more of my time." I turned around.

Hamilton glowering at Stone. "Let's leave." He offered me his arm.

I swung around again to face Stone. "And how dare you be so rude." I felt my voice waver. I really had no idea why the man would ask me up there to simply insult me. "Unless you're going to arrest me again for something I have not done, I shall bid you a good evening!" I nearly shouted the last words then turned around to leave the place.

"It wasn't I who asked you to come," Stone said in a steady voice.

I hesitated, then swung around to see him give what looked like a half smile. *Surely not*, I thought. *Is the man deranged?*

"It was Mrs Flint," Stone said.

I regarded him for a moment, feeling he was enjoying our exchange. "Are you referring to Mrs Ina Flint of Millar's Hotel?"

"The same. She wants you – an amateur – to act on her behalf in her defence." The small smile spread across his face as if in slow motion. "She's been arrested for the murder of Michel Blanc."

"Are you serious?" I put my hands on my hips.

Stone raised his eyebrows and looked me up and down in a most disagreeable fashion as if I was acting in a manner below my station. "I think you should calm down, you'll end up as deranged as she is."

"She is not deranged," I said. "She's a hard-working woman."

"She has a history of obsessions for certain men. And it was her scarf used as the murder weapon."

I felt a chill run up my neck and let out a slow breath. As I stared at him, I knew that I could no longer ignore the death of Michel Blanc.

CHAPTER 6

*P*C Ryan showed me to the cell where Mrs Flint was being held. Hamilton was asked to remain in the waiting area.

"For what it's worth," Ryan whispered. "I don't think Ina's guilty. She's been friends with my mum for years. She turned up at the hotel when Stone had just arrived and he recognised her. Then when he realised it was her scarf that was used to strangle the Frenchman, he arrested her on the spot. Chambers protested, but he told us he's in charge and sent Chambers off to sort out a petty thief who'd stolen a loaf of bread."

"I'd rather not be involved, especially as I assured Sergeant Chambers that I would not be. But I can't let Mrs Flint take the blame for something she didn't do."

Ryan opened the hatch of the cell door. "You have a visitor, Ina." He opened the door and let me in.

"Oh, my goodness, thank you so much for coming." She wept as she struggled to stand from the bench.

"Remain seated, Mrs Flint – I'll sit with you," I said in a calm voice.

"I didn't do it. You have to believe me, my lady."

"If course you didn't. It's quite obvious that you would not have collected a scarf if you had indeed used it to murder a man. You would have taken it with you and disposed of it."

"So the killer wants me to take the blame?" She wiped her eyes. "Who would do such a thing?"

The hatch of the door opened. "I'm taking you to an interview room," Stone said in a gruff voice. "Keep away from the door."

Ryan walked in with a pair of hand cuffs and mouthed *sorry* to Mrs Flint as he cuffed her.

"Is this really necessary?" I asked as I left the room to find Stone outside.

"Follow me," he said without comment.

We were soon in the interview room which I had been summoned to before on a couple of occasions. It was dingy and unwelcoming with dark green walls.

I sat with Mrs Flint and Inspector Stone sat opposite us as PC Ryan guarded the door.

Stone flipped over his notebook. "We have interviewed the staff at The Grand Hotel and have also taken a statement from your husband, Mr Douglas Flint."

"You've been to my house?" Mrs Flint asked.

"Correct. And I have deduced the following." He took a deep breath as if preparing to make a speech. "On Sunday evening, you cooked a meal for your husband and then poured him a large glass of brandy." He used a monotone voice. "When he became tired, you suggested he go to bed. You helped the drowsy man upstairs. When he was asleep, you changed your clothing and snuck out of the house, unbeknownst to him."

Mrs Flint did not comment, so I assumed the Inspector was recalling truc events.

"You then met the victim, Michel Blanc at The Grand Hotel – alone, in the ballroom."

"Michel Blanc gave private dance lessons on a Sunday evening," I said. "He would have been alone with anyone seeking individual tuition."

Stone stared at me but made no comment before turning to face Mrs Flint and continuing: "You stran-gled Michel Blanc to death with the scarf matching your dress." He lifted two items. A blue dress in one hand, and in the other a scarf cut from what appeared to be the same cloth. He had clearly collected the dress from her house.

"I didn't strangle him," Mrs Flint said. "I could never do that to anyone."

"And then as if to fool us into thinking you were innocent, you turned up today asking if the murder weapon was in lost property." Stone paused and put the tips of his fingers together. "Very clever, but the bluff did not fool the police."

"That's not true!" Mrs Flint said, and fumbled with her handkerchief with her cuffed hands, attempting to wipe her eyes.

"Why did you not tell your husband that you were leaving the house?" Stone asked her.

Mrs Flint licked her lips but did not reply.

Stone continued: "Do you deny drugging the man so he would not know you were gone?"

"He was not drugged! He often feels drowsy after a large meal and a brandy," she said.

"And in that knowledge, you ensured he would be unaware of your absence. And he would have thought you at home all evening and provided you with the alibi you needed to cover your crime. I repeat, why did you conceal your absence from the house?"

"I wanted to take dance lessons. Mr Flint would have created a fuss."

"It's hardly surprising that a husband would object to his wife meeting another man alone, at night." Stone glared at her. "Do you not respect your wedding vows? To honour and obey?"

"Inspector Stone," I said. "We are in an age of suffrage. Mrs Flint is permitted to undertake whatever activities she chooses without permission from her husband."

Stone ignored me. "I noted during my investigations at Millar's Hotel earlier this year, that you have an obsession with Gilbert Barry."

"It's not an obsession, Inspector," I said, feeling the need to interject. "Mrs Flint is merely a fan of his music and acting skills, and now he is a family friend of hers."

"As you say – a fanatic," Stone said. "And Mr Flint is

not pleased. He was shocked that we had arrested you but blamed himself, admitting that he should have put a stop to your obsessions much sooner. Poor man, *he* apologised for *your* actions."

"You told him I'm a killer?" Mrs Flint said in a mere whisper.

"Innocent, until proven guilty, Inspector Stone," I said. "It's most irresponsible, I would say, to tell Mr Flint his wife strangled a man. The poor fellow must be beside himself." I put a comforting arm around Ina, then looked back at the Inspector.

"Please explain, Mrs Flint, why you left home and met Michel Blanc," Inspector Stone asked.

"I've a trip booked, to Torquay, in three weeks. My Joe, he plays piano for Gilbert Barry and Mae Grey. Douglas doesn't want to go. The last time I saw them at a show in Eastbourne, Gilbert asked me to promise him a dance. It's not a romance. He's happily married to the sweetest woman. I just wanted to learn a waltz so that I didn't embarrass my Joe."

"That sounds entirely reasonable," I said, feeling immensely sorry that Mrs Flint felt so embarrassed by her dancing that she had slipped out of the house. I would have happily taught her myself, had I known.

"I've been so happy, travelling to see my son." Mrs Flint hiccupped. "I'm so proud of him."

"Joe would not be embarrassed I'm sure," I said in a comforting voice.

"I know, I was being silly, I guess I –"

The Inspector interrupted her. "The night of the murder. Your movements please."

"I left the house as soon as Douglas was asleep and went down to the hotel. I reached the ballroom and heard voices as soon as I opened the door."

"To whom was Michel speaking?" I asked.

"A woman, she was shorter than me, so about five feet with tied-back brown hair, wearing a blue coat. She was talking to Michel and said: 'If you don't come back to London, it'll be the end of Michel Blanc.'"

"This woman threatened him?" I asked.

Mrs Flint nodded. "He called after her, but she left."

"What did he say to her?" I asked.

"He called her name – Rose."

Inspector Stone made notes. "Continue."

"Michel made no comment as the woman passed me by. She was flushed and looked as if she was going to cry. I felt sorry for her. Then his expression changed, and he smiled at me as if nothing had happened. He gave me my lesson and the scarf I had around my neck was getting in the way, so he suggested I remove it – which I did. Then after my lesson, I left and forgot to take my scarf." Mrs Flint paused and watched Stone making notes. Then she turned to me. "It was my first lesson, but I'll be honest, Doug was right, I can't dance. The last time I waltzed was at our wedding when I trod on his foot. He's never let me forget it. He would have made fun of me having lessons, that's why I didn't tell him. Not to deceive him. I didn't want to be ridiculed."

She turned back to the Inspector. "I appreciate how it looks from the outside."

"Did you see anyone else at the hotel?" I asked her.

"Leave the questioning to me," Stone said, then turned to Mrs Flint. "Answer."

"When I came out of the ballroom, the rest of the hotel was quiet. It wasn't until this morning that I realised I'd left my scarf there. As you know, I went to the hotel to collect it and then you arrested me."

"This all seems clear, don't you think, Inspector?" I said.

"She's not going to admit to murder, is she?" he growled whilst gesturing at Mrs Flint in an ungentlemanly manner.

"Can you please arrange for Mrs Flint's release," I said.

"I'm afraid I cannot do that unless there's compelling evidence to show she's innocent. She was the last person to see Michel Blanc alive, and her scarf was used to strangle him." He stood up. "I will of course continue my enquires in order to bring the matter to a satisfactory conclusion." He gestured at Ryan who was still standing by the door. "Take her back to the cell."

"No, no, please I can't stand it in there!" Mrs Flint wept. "I want to go home."

"Inspector Stone, this woman is distressed and clearly innocent."

"So say many defenders of murderers," he said, closing his notebook.

"In that case, I will discover exactly what went on here," I said.

"Of course you will," he said in a sarcastic tone, but he paused. I saw a flicker in his eye which I could not quite comprehend.

I felt dreadful as Ryan helped a sobbing Mrs Flint back to the cell. At least the younger man was sympathetic. I resolved to ensure Douglas Flint would be told the truth. *The poor fellow,* I thought. *He's been left thinking his wife is a murderer!*

I WALKED BACK at the hotel with Hamilton, advising him of what had transpired in the interview room.

"So much for a peaceful time together," I said with a sigh.

"As long as we're together," he said.

My face flushed as he offered me his arm. "As much as I wanted a rest, I've grown rather fond of Mrs Flint, and keeping her safe overrides any selfish feelings of my own."

"I fully understand," Hamilton said, although he seemed rather eager. "But you are far from selfish, Ellen."

When we reached the hotel, Lottie was exiting the dining room with the Simpson sisters and the Major. "What happened?" she asked.

"Mrs Flint has been charged with murder." I explained that she was the woman who had left her scarf in the ballroom. "So we're now officially investigating, to clear her name. The poor woman is distraught."

"Poor Ina," Lottie said.

"If there's anything we can do to help?" Betty asked.

I was sure I heard Hamilton give a low groan.

I smiled at Betty. "You have a keen eye. I may well be asking for your insights. But for now, I need to eat as I'm famished, and I'm sure Captain Hamilton is also hungry."

After the Simpson sisters and the Major had retired to the cards room, Lottie and I went up to my suite and Hamilton visited the restaurant to order food to be delivered for us.

As we ate, I updated Lottie on my visit to the police station in detail. She recorded everything on some writing paper which she planned to transcribe into a new notebook – one she planned to purchase the following morning whilst taking Prince for his walk.

"Who are our suspects?" she asked.

"We have a few, by the sounds of it," Hamilton said.

"That man who owns the pier is top of my list," Lottie said. "The look on his face!"

"Indeed," I said. "Let's discuss Richard Sheringham."

Lottie wrote his name down.

I continued: "His actions suggested he feared his wife was having an affair with Michel Blanc."

"She probably was from what we saw," Lottie said. "The way he kissed her neck!"

"A motive for murder," Hamilton said.

"Her name's Violet Sheringham," Lottie said as she wrote it on the page. "She slapped Michel across the face."

"We need to discover why," I said. "As a top priority."

"A trip to the pier may be in order," Hamilton said.

"Then there's that other dancer man," Lottie said. "The drunk one. Herbert...Lightfoot," she said slowly as she wrote his name.

"A man who believes his livelihood was stolen from him by Michel," I said.

"Another clear motive," Hamilton added.

"And Eddie, the barman," Lottie said. "He seems really nice but Michel didn't like him. Well, from what we saw. When he grabbed him from across the bar."

"I hate to speak ill of the dead," I said. "But it's apparent that Michel Blanc was unpopular."

"A thoroughly unlikeable chap, by the sounds of the way he treated you," Hamilton said. "We have four clear suspects."

"And there's a fifth, Rose," I added, now feeling fully immersed in the case. "She was with Michel when Mrs Flint arrived for her lesson. She's from London and asked him to return otherwise he would no longer exist!"

"It would be helpful if we could locate her," Hamilton said. "But with only her Christian name, we do not have much to go on. London is a rather large town."

"Well, it sounds like she said she'd kill him, so maybe she should be the top suspect," Lottie said, underlining her name.

"We should find out what other students he had that day. They may have seen her arrive," I said.

"We'll have our work cut out, interviewing all of these people, considering we are not known to them," Hamilton said.

"The first thing I wish to do is visit Mr Flint to assure him that his wife is innocent!" I said.

"The poor chap must be suffering from shock," Hamilton said.

"I also suggest we speak to the chef, because he's French. He's likely to have background information on Michel and whereabouts in France he came from. If I happen upon any details, I will pass that information to Chambers as he'll have the task of informing his family back in France, and maybe they will travel here, to make the necessary arrangements."

"Ellen, with family in France, this case will take longer than the days we have left in Branden Bay," Hamilton said with a frown.

"I can't return to Ashcombe and leave Mrs Flint in the cells." I caught Hamilton's grave expression. "But of course, Ernest, you must fulfil your contract and leave for Cairo as soon as you receive your instructions."

"We'll have to work hard on this one and I intend to help you whilst I still can," Hamilton said.

"Lottie, whilst we're with Mr Flint tomorrow, could you please ask Betty and Nelly about Michel and all of our suspects?" I said. "Their sharp eyes may have noticed something we've missed. Also, ask if they've met anyone named Rose."

CHAPTER 7

"*You* ou look nice," Lottie said as I checked my reflection in the mirror. After spending four months away from Ashcombe Hall, I was used to dressing myself and styling my own hair. It was lucky that my maid back in Ashcombe had married and was soon to be with child, as I would have needed to find her alternative work. I could no longer imagine having anyone help me dress, unless it was to assist with an awkward fastening.

"We will be busy today," I said. "I want to ensure my makeup stays in place, as I wish us to speak to as many of the suspects as we can."

"Really?" Lottie said, raising her eyebrows. "I thought you might be looking so nice because of Ernest."

"Of course not," I said quickly, though I knew she was completely correct. I'd made a little more effort with my appearance since Hamilton had arrived at the hotel. I had to admit, I was not only acting like a thoroughly modern woman, I was looking like one as well. "And you look lovely too," I added, trying to shift the focus away from myself.

She smiled back at me. "Hopefully Sebastian will be back soon. I wonder if he's got my letters."

"They may well have arrived in Mayfair, but it's possible his mother intercepted them," I said.

"It wouldn't surprise me," she said. Lady Bandberry had offered Lottie a place at a school in Switzerland on the understanding that she would no longer see Sebastian. Lottie had of course refused, but she now knew she was unlikely to ever be accepted by Sebastian's family.

"In Sebastian's letter, he made no reference to the letters I'd sent him and said he was looking forward to hearing from me," she said. "I've started to save them up and I'll give them to him when he comes back. Well –" she paused "– if comes back."

"I'm sure he will, and at least when he attends university, he'll be free of his scheming mother," I said. "And all of your letters will reach him."

Prince lolloped over to me wagging his tail and nudged my hand which was his way of telling me he wanted a walk.

I stroked his silky red fur. "Don't worry, boy, Lottie will take you out after we've eaten breakfast."

"I'll get his bone out for when we're downstairs," Lottie said.

We had arranged to meet Hamilton in the restaurant for breakfast, and ten minutes later, as we walked through the reception and passed the hotel bar, I spotted Eddie cleaning glasses.

I whispered to Lottie, "Let's take this opportunity to have a quick word with the barman." I wandered over with Lottie by my side.

"You would like a drink?" he asked us with a grin.

"It's a little early," I said with a smile. "I wanted to have a quick word."

"About what, my lady?"

"It's a nasty business isn't it, with the French dancer?" I said.

Eddie gave his head a slow nod. "He obviously upset the wrong woman. I hear the one that done it is inside the cells. Apparently, she's a bit older than his usual type. She must have pots of money."

I frowned. "I have to inform you that the woman in the cells is certainly not the murderer."

"Ah, a friend of yours, is she?" He paused and narrowed his eyes. "Of course, you like investigating murders. I heard all about it." He placed the glass he was cleaning on the bar and leaned forward, giving me a cheeky grin. "Are you interrogating me?"

"I'm simply defending a friend. That is all."

"Just because she's a friend don't mean she never done it." He straightened up and placed the glass on a rack. "But if you don't think she did it, you'll need to find who did."

"Exactly," I said.

"She didn't do it," Lottie said. "I've known her for a while. She'd never do a thing like that."

"Poor woman," Eddie said with a sigh. "There's nothing more important than freedom." He looked me in the eye. "But if it was her that done it, I wouldn't blame her. Michel made many a woman mad."

"We noticed," Lottie said. "That Violet Sheringham slapped his face on Saturday."

"He deserved it." Eddie picked up another glass to polish. "He was unkind to her."

"In what way?" I asked. "What upset did he cause?"

Eddie regarded me for a moment before he continued. "I don't know, exactly. But he also deserved a slap from her husband. Carrying on like that in front of him."

"Do you know what his relationship was with Mrs Sheringham?" I asked.

"Violet has a magic about her, it's as if they're all under her spell. I don't know if there was anything between them. Not really."

"What about you?" I asked.

Eddie laughed. "I'm nearer her age than Michel was, and her husband's old enough to be her old man. But no, I've never been under her spell."

"So, if you had to guess who done it, who would it be?" Lottie asked.

He looked about him then back to us and lowered his voice. "On Sunday morning, I went for a walk and saw Michel with Herbert Lightfoot. They were having a row.

Herbert pulled his arm back as if he was gonna punch his lights out, and he's a big bloke." He took a breath. "Michel stepped back with his hands up and told Herbert that his bad times were his own fault. And he pointed at him and said – 'You're fat and you can't dance.'"

"Did Lightfoot punch him then?" Lottie asked.

"No, it was odd. Lightfoot hung his head and walked away. I felt sorry for him, but maybe he hit back later when he'd had time to think on it, to get mad about it." He looked around him again and lowered his voice. "And Lightfoot had an obsession with Violet too." He straightened up. "A big one."

Lottie leaned on the bar and wrote the information down on some paper she had retrieved from her bag, so fast I wondered whether the handwriting would be legible.

"What exactly led to Mr Lightfoot's job being given to Michel?" I asked.

"He'd been drinking too much. Some say it was 'cause he wanted what he couldn't have."

"You mean Violet?"

"It's just what I heard. And he was ill too many times. Angus asked Micky to fill in for him."

"You mean Michel?" I said.

Eddie ran a hand through his hair. "Yeah. I called him that to wind him up a couple of times. He didn't like it, though. Got really mad when I did."

"Did you often make him mad?" I asked.

"I guess so."

"He dragged you across the bar Saturday night, why was that?" Lottie asked.

Eddie straightened up. "I just told him he was losing his touch with women. Bad timing I guess, him having just been slapped by Violet."

"I understand Michel came to Branden Bay as part of a travelling show over at the music hall?" I said.

"Yeah, he came over here one night and danced with Pearl, standing in for Lightfoot when he was laid up. Mr Scott offered him the job on the spot, he stayed in town and lived here at The Grand and poor old Lightfoot got kicked out." He polished another glass. "I'd only been here a week myself." He sighed. "I'll be moving on soon. This place has got an evil vibe about it now. And the town's had four murders in as many months."

"How did Mr Lightfoot react to losing his job?" I asked.

"He went downhill quick over the past two months. He was an 'alf-decent looking bloke. Yeah, he carried a bit of weight, but nothing like the mess he is today. He lost a job at the pier too. He's now at the music hall as an usher, but he'll get the sack from there if he don't watch out and he's already skint."

"How does he afford to drink at the bar with limited funds?" I asked.

Eddie shrugged. "Dunno. And it's not my problem." He took a deep breath. "It brings it home, don't it, when people die. My brother died in the war." He stood up straight and smiled. "That's why we have to live each day with a smile, in case it's our last."

I could see past the smile and viewed the sadness in his eyes. I knew that his sentiment, of living for the day, was behind a lot of the party culture of the youth and the Bright Young Things.

"Lady Ellen."

I turned to find Angus Scott approaching the bar. "We're closing the ballroom for a two nights out of respect for the deceased. So, I've asked Eddie to stock this bar which will be busier over the next couple of days."

"We were talking to Eddie about Michel," I said. "But we will leave him to his work now. Sorry for disturbing him."

We walked out of the bar and Angus accompanied us. "I'm most surprised at Mrs Flint," Angus said. "Dora has always spoken well of her."

I remembered that Mrs Flint used to work in the children's home where Angus's wife was brought up.

"She often viewed Mrs Flint as family. It will not go down well with her when she returns. Do you think the Inspector has got it right?" he asked me.

"Absolutely not! She's clearly innocent," I said. "I've visited Mrs Flint. I'm quite sure it was not her. Although the Inspector will not release her. Unfortunately, Inspector Stone is the type of detective who wishes to have at least one person in the cell when he's investigating."

"This is such a stressful matter. I don't know what has happened to the bay this year. I guess with the influx of new guests, these sorts of instances occur. And if it's not Mrs Flint, then the murderer could still be at large. Do you think they might be staying here, in my hotel?"

"That's what we intend to find out," Lottie said, waving the paper she'd been making notes on.

Angus raised his eyebrows. "So, you'll be investigating after all?"

"I have no choice with Mrs Flint behind bars," I said with a sigh. "I can't leave her to face this alone."

"That's reassuring for me. I'm visiting Dora at the hospital today to plan her return. She will be coming home a week on Friday. Please do keep me abreast of the situation, and I'll inform my staff to be extra vigilant and to report anything they see that is suspicious to your good selves."

"That's an excellent idea, Mr Scott," I said.

Angus hurried away.

I made my way to the breakfast room with Lottie.

As we entered, Betty waved at us and I saw she was seated next to the Major, with her sister on his other side. Hamilton scowled from beside Nelly. I had to keep my lips firmly together as I found his dislike for them quite amusing. Knowing Hamilton's opinion on gossip, I knew exactly why they grated upon his nerves.

"Have you had any more thoughts about the murder?" Nelly asked as we took our seats.

"I have indeed, and wanted to gather your valued opinions." I smiled at her and then to Betty.

"It's so exciting that you're investigating," Betty said, clutching her hands together.

"I'm involved only to clear Mrs Flint's name. If I find a secure alibi for her, I will leave the rest of the matter to the police."

"I guess his family will be coming over from France," Nelly said.

"Do you know whereabouts in France he's from?" I asked them.

"We asked him that," Betty said. "He just said the north."

"We were wondering about the barman, Eddie. On Saturday night, Michel grabbed him over the bar by the scruff of his neck," Lottie said.

"Outrageous!" the Major said.

"Do you know Eddie well?" I asked the sisters.

"Oh yes, he sometimes has a drink late on and we chat to him as he cleans the bar down. He's never had much nice to say about Michel. Said he was a fraud and had a bad reputation with women."

"A reputation with anyone in particular?" I asked.

Betty shrugged. "Nelly and I will find out more." She nodded at her sister. "We love Eddie though, I can't imagine he would hurt a fly. But we can find things out from him. Once he's had a few drinks, he likes to gossip just as much as we do." She laughed.

"We often saw Michel and Eddie talking in hushed tones," Nelly said. "They clearly were not fond of each other, but I would not be surprised if Michel was caught up in something shady." She pursed her lips and sat back in her chair.

"I think it's more likely to be a chap who killed him," Hamilton said. "Rather than a woman. The killer was probably engaged in an argument with Michel, saw Mrs Flint's scarf and used it on the spur of the moment."

Major Fitzwilliam nodded. "Agreed."

The waitress took our breakfast orders and then replenished the tea and coffee pots.

"Did you three notice anything on Sunday night?" I asked. "Where were you at the hotel that evening?"

"We're in the cards room every evening," Betty said. "Playing with Wally." She looked longingly at the Major.

The Major's face changed to a deep red, maybe at being addressed in such an affectionate manner, and nodded with a smile at Betty. "A pleasure."

"I wonder whether you happened to see a petite woman with brown tied-back hair, wearing a navy coat?" I asked them. "When our friend, Mrs Flint turned up for her lesson, a woman of that description named Rose was leaving the ballroom."

Nelly frowned. "I'm not sure."

"I don't know anyone at the hotel called Rose," Betty said.

"And have you spoken to the police?" Lottie asked.

"The police didn't speak to us at all," Nelly said with a shake of her head. "They dragged that poor woman, your Mrs Flint, away in handcuffs and abandoned their questioning."

"Thank goodness you're in town, a super sleuth," Betty gushed. "I must confess, we read all about your other cases in the newspaper."

Hamilton huffed as he turned the page on his own newspaper.

I changed the subject, a little embarrassed. "Tell us about Herbert Lightfoot."

"Vulgar!" the Major said.

"He curses too much," Nelly said. "I think that's what Walter means."

"Absolutely" Major Fitzwilliam confirmed.

"He lacks class," Nelly added.

"He's much better during the day though, isn't he?" Betty said to her sister.

"Before he's drunk himself to a stupor," Nelly said with a huff.

Our food arrived and we discussed less contentious issues. Nelly told us about how she loved the cinema, and about the film Sherlock Jr which starred Buster Keaton and was currently showing at the Branden Bay Plaza.

"You must take Lady Ellen to see it, Captain Hamilton," Betty said.

I blushed as I looked at Hamilton, not knowing whether Betty was matchmaking or whether she assumed we were a couple.

"It's a great idea," Lottie said. "I could go with Sebastian when he gets back. We could all go together."

Hamilton, having finished his breakfast, touched his folded newspaper on the table as if he was waiting for us to finish eating so that he could return to it.

"Another divorce?" Betty said, pointing to the newspaper. "It seems there's one every week these days."

"That's due to last year's Matrimonial Causes Act." Hamilton tapped the newspaper. "There have been a few high-profile cases."

"Which," I added, "is not a bad thing. Women are now permitted to petition for divorce on account of adultery as well as men!"

Betty sighed. "It's a shame so many men are unfaithful to their wives."

"Disgraceful," Fitzwilliam said.

"There are still women tied to their husbands, though," I said. "Because they cannot afford the process, or would be left penniless."

Nelly pointed to the newspaper. "Is there anything about the Vigilante Slasher?"

"Not for a week," Hamilton said nonchalantly.

"Who do you think he is?" Lottie asked.

"I doubt we'll ever know," Hamilton said.

"He's always one step ahead of the police," Nelly said. "He's much too intelligent for them."

I felt uneasy thinking of the Vigilante Slasher. He managed to track down the crooks who evaded the police and, after killing them, he slashed a cross into their left arm. He had killed a pair of crooks in nearby Bristol, and caught up with a thief in London. It was a thief I had alerted the police to. There had been a worry at the back of my mind, that the Slasher was someone I had met, as few people were aware of that particular theft. But I had pushed it from my mind as a pure coincidence, because as well as being a thief that particular person had other vices that could have resulted in a visit from the Slasher, who in this case had spared them after removing a lock of hair.

After breakfast had concluded, my mind swam with the enormity of the fact-finding mission we'd taken on. A man whose family lived in France, a woman called Rose who lived in London who we had no hope of tracking down, with only a Christian name to go on. All we could do would be to work with the suspects in town.

Lottie walked ahead of us as Hamilton and I took the stairs.

"This case feels tougher than the previous ones, does it not?" he said.

"As you said, we're not known to most of the suspects," I said. "It's difficult to broach the subject of the strangling with them when we're not acquainted and of course, do not have the powers of the police."

"I'm sure you'll succeed, you're so warm, welcoming and easy to speak to." He smiled at me. "And you have Lottie and myself to help."

We reached the top of the stairs and Hamilton stopped and looked into my eyes. "I'm happy to escort you to the cinema this evening, if you would like me to."

I smiled at him. "I would like that very much."

CHAPTER 8

*H*amilton and I were soon walking up the path to the front door of the Flint family home. It was a Victorian style house in a row of terraces.

Hamilton pulled the heavy door knocker and tapped it twice.

I looked to the upper floors when there was no immediate answer, and saw a curtain move. "Perhaps we're a little early for a house call?" I was about to suggest we left when the door swung open.

Mr Flint stood before us. He was a handsome man with a tanned face, dark hair with grey flecks, a strong jawline and a dimple in his chin, although he looked rather dishevelled. He wore trousers with his shirt undone enough so that I could see his vest. He narrowed his eyes. "You the press?"

"Good morning, Mr Flint," Hamilton said. "We're

good friends of your lady wife, Mrs Ina Flint, and she has asked Lady Ellen to help clear her name."

"Huh!" he said. "You'll have a job on your hands with this one." He shook his head. "The police warned me about you poking your nose in."

"Inspector Stone does not approve of me," I said. "But I have Ina's best interests at heart."

"You best come in." He hoisted up the braces attached to his trousers, which had been hanging by his thighs, and pulled them over his shoulders, then gestured for us to follow him.

The lounge was a little untidy with unwashed glasses and discarded bottles of alcohol on several surfaces. I put my hand beneath my nose as I noticed an ashtray full of cigarette butts, which gave off a stale aroma and required emptying. As we sat down, we heard a door close with a bang, which must have been caught in the breeze. Hamilton turned his head and looked out of the bay window and I glanced over his shoulder to see the back of a woman opening the gate who had dark brown hair.

"The cleaner," Mr Flint said in a gruff voice. "I've had lots of help, food packages and well wishes. No one can believe what Ina did to me, and that bloke she strangled. Mind you, he had it coming to him, seems he was romancing many in Branden Bay and only the married ones." He plonked himself in an armchair.

I'd visited Mrs Flint some weeks before and recognised the lounge, although it had been a lot tidier. Upon the wall in the corner had been a framed portrait of Gilbert Barry. The portrait was missing, but I noticed the edge of a picture frame in the waste bin.

"Mr Flint," I said. "We're here to reassure you that Ina is completely innocent."

He leaned forward. "Are they letting her out?"

"Well," I said slowly. "Not yet."

He sat back in his chair. "What you mean to say is that you *think* she's innocent. Do the police still reckon she done it?"

"Yes," Hamilton said. "But, they have it wrong."

"You're bound to say that, you're friends with her. But you don't know her, not like I do."

"I can assure you of her innocence," I said.

"I have personal experience of being wrongly arrested by Inspector Stone," Hamilton said. "The man, I have to say, is a complete buffoon."

"It's our job," I said, "to provide evidence to show that your wife is innocent so that she can return home to you. I would like to ask you about her movements that night."

"Of course." He took a deep breath. "Like I told that inspector, she cooked a stew. She served it late as she'd been bathing. It was Sunday evening, so I thought it was unusual. Not unusual that she was in the bath, she always takes a bath on a Sunday. Nothing new there. But unusual that she made me an evening meal – that wasn't usual. Normally I get a cold meat sandwich with what's left over from Sunday lunch. But I didn't complain, the stew was nice. She gave me a large portion and it sent me right to sleep it did. 'Go up early, Doug,' she'd said. Like she really cared." He shook his head. "She just wanted me asleep while she went off with her fancy man. Then killed the poor fella."

"Of course she cares about you." I leaned forward. "Ina has killed no one."

"And Mr Flint, your wife was not a lover of Michel Blanc," Hamilton said in a stern voice.

"I guess he wasn't interested," Mr Flint continued, as if we'd made no comment whatsoever. "She used to be a beautiful girl when I met her, but now, well…she's no oil painting is she!"

"Mr Flint," Hamilton said. "Your wife is indeed a most handsome woman."

"Oh, she's been throwing her charms at you too, has she?"

I was beginning to dislike Mr Flint. "Ina simply wished to take dance classes which she found embarrassing to mention to you." I pursed my lips as I regarded him. "That's the truth of the matter."

"I guess the bloke didn't want her," he said. "So she finished him off."

The man appeared to have accepted his wife's guilt and I realised I had a job on my hands to convince him otherwise.

"Why on earth do you think your wife committed murder?" Hamilton said. "That Mrs Flint is capable of such a thing?"

"That Inspector told me, didn't he. He pointed out that she's been obsessed with another fella before." He gestured at the waste bin. "Gilbert Barry. Since she's met his wife, who's a right looker, and realised there was no hope, she moved on to Michel Blanc." He sighed and spoke in a quiet voice. "I'm shocked. It's cut me to the core this has. My Ina a cold-blooded killer!"

Oh dear, I thought. "Ina would not have gone to the hotel to look for her scarf had she'd known it was a murder weapon."

"She would have taken it with her and destroyed the evidence," Hamilton added. "And certainly not walked into the path of the police. Mr Flint, you must know that your wife is not capable of such a thing?"

"She's been totally different since she was left that money," he said in a quiet voice. "Taken the grey out of her hair, had it cut, got new clothes."

"What money?" Hamilton asked.

"Ah," I said. "The money that James Millar left her." The deceased owner of Millar's hotel had left Mrs Flint a generous two thousand pounds in his will.

"She's got trips booked to go and watch our Joe in travelling music shows. Huh, all I got was a box of cigars, and I don't even smoke the things. I prefer me gaspers." He gestured to the stubs of the strong-smelling cigarettes.

I managed to catch his gaze. "From what I hear, your wife has worked hard for years, at the children's home, then during the war when she was with the fire service. And she works many hours a day up at Millar's hotel."

"I bet they've given her the sack now," Mr Flint said. "Not only is she never there, she's killed a man."

"They're refurbishing the hotel. I would have thought there's not much call for a housekeeping manager at this time," Hamilton said.

"I would have thought it fitting for her to treat herself a little," I said. "Having come into some money, after working hard for many years."

"By flaunting herself in clothes that are not for a decent wife in her fortieth year? Making a fool of herself, dancing late at night with strangers? Many folks have been commenting on her to me."

I bet they have, I thought. They were no doubt jealous of Mrs Flint's new financial position. Although I'd visited the house with the intention of informing Mr Flint that he need not worry about his wife going to the gallows, I was beginning to see that as well as Inspector Stone's words, Branden Bay's gossip had already dug its claws deeply into him.

"What time was it on Monday that you went to bed?" I asked, thinking it better to gather evidence to convince him of her innocence.

"I've no idea."

"And what time did your wife go to bed?" I added.

"Don't know that either, she slept in the spare room. Said she'd been up reading late and didn't want to wake me. Huh! Reading? How am I supposed to believe that she's telling the truth now she says she's innocent, when all she does is lie?"

"Mr Flint," Hamilton said. "I know you must feel shocked at having been told by the police that your wife has committed a crime. And there's no denying that she slipped out of the house to learn how to dance. But could you please take a breath and consider the position with a clear mind. Your wife is no killer!"

Mr Flint leaned back in his chair. "I'm sorry. You're right, it's been a real shock. That Inspector Stone was sure she'd done it."

I did not feel Mr Flint was in the right frame of mind for any further questions. "Once you've thought on the matter, you may wish to visit Ina, to give her your support," I suggested. "As soon as you see her, you'll know she's innocent. And hopefully, she'll be back here with you very soon."

"Do you really think that?" he asked in a small voice.

"Absolutely, and she needs you now," I said.

He blinked and gave his head a slow nod. "Thanks for coming."

We bade him farewell and walked down the slope to the promenade.

"He seems pretty sure Mrs Flint strangled Michel Blanc," Hamilton said with a grim expression.

"I'm assuming Inspector Stone was convincing when he visited."

"Mrs Flint needs all the moral support she can get," Hamilton said. "I hope he pays his wife a visit soon."

"Hopefully our words have sown the seed of doubt in Inspector Stone's accusations."

"It's not the only strangulation reported this year," he said. "There have been a couple of reports in the newspaper, the most notable of which was a solved crime which surrounded the death of the owner of Taverham shoes. Mr Taverham had an affair, his mistress was found guilty and is in prison. There was also another killing of a man in Eastbourne a few weeks ago. His wife is suspected as he committed adultery. He'd been spotted with a brunette the day he died."

I pondered on this as we took the stroll back along the promenade, hoping that recent changes in the law would encourage women to divorce their husbands rather than kill them. I watched those walking along the sands appearing carefree, and wished that could have been Hamilton and myself. That we could have been afforded some time to relax, rather than being tied up in this matter. Although I also realised that Hamilton appeared to be thoroughly enjoying the investigation.

"I will do my best to ensure we have a pleasant day," Hamilton said, and as he smiled at me, I felt incredibly warm.

As we entered the hotel, the Simpson sisters and Major Fitzwilliam were again playing cards. Betty saw me looking at them and waved at us.

Hamilton groaned.

I, on the other hand, I could not help but smile as soon as I spotted them, as they did so lighten the atmosphere – which was rather gloomy, considering recent events.

The receptionist gave Hamilton a quick wave.

"I appear to have received a message," he said and

went to the reception desk. I guessed he was relieved to avoid Betty and Nelly.

I walked into the cards room.

"How's the investigation going?" Betty whispered when I reached their table.

"We've visited Mr Flint to assure him the police have their facts wrong – the man was in a bit of a mess."

"Not surprising," Nelly said.

Betty nodded. "Can't have been easy, being told his wife has been accused of murder."

"It appears the police were pretty convincing," I said.

"Surely the police will let her go soon?" Betty said with her eyebrows raised. "It's obviously not her."

"Ridiculous," the Major said.

"What do you propose to do next?" Nelly asked.

"We're going to the pier," I said, then instantly regretted at as excitement passed over Betty's face.

"We're going to the tea dance today, as well, aren't we?" Betty said.

"Absolutely," the Major said.

"Only to watch," Nelly added.

"We could all go together," Betty said as Hamilton returned.

I was hoping to go over with just Lottie and Hamilton. But I didn't have an excuse to give them, and the pier was of course a public place. "Yes, of course. We'll meet you at two o'clock in the reception after luncheon."

"Splendid!" Fitzwilliam said with a satisfied nod.

I heard Hamilton sigh as we left the cards room and I turned to him. "Sorry, I should have thought before I spoke! I take it you're not overly keen on the trio?"

"I have to say Ellen, I hope I'm not being too bold. But I do hanker after time which we two can spend together before I set sail. And I've just collected a message that I must travel to London tomorrow."

My heart skipped a beat. Would this be our last evening together? "This evening, I would love for us to see the film at the Plaza. We could share a meal together, beforehand?"

His face lit up and as he gazed into my eyes, I was convinced that there was so much unspoken between us. I was aware yet again of the letter inside my handbag. My cheeks felt hot.

He offered me his arm as we approached the stairs.

CHAPTER 9

*T*he salty tang of the sea air greeted us as we arrived at the shoreside of the pier. The wooden planks beneath our feet creaked as we headed for the main pier building. The sun was shining, lighting up the sandy beach that curved along the bay. Seagulls cried and waves lapped against the struts of the pier as we walked along it.

Hamilton looked every bit the dashing gentleman, his fair hair slicked back, his attire as always impeccable, despite the casual seaside setting. I felt as if I was savouring each moment we had left together. Ahead of us, I noticed other couples strolling hand in hand, and blushed at the thought of doing that with Hamilton. Behind us, the Simpson sisters followed arm in arm with Major Fitzwilliam, their matching gold-rimmed glasses glinting in the sunlight. Lottie walked beside them and held onto Prince's leash, as he appeared to wish to sniff everything and everyone with excitement, having been cooped up for too long in the room whilst Lottie had transcribed her notes into a new notebook. She had purchased it whilst we had been with Mr Flint.

I heard the occasional snippets of conversation carried on the wind as the Simpson sisters questioned Lottie about Sebastian. The Major nodded along, interjecting with single word comments. I wished I'd warned Lottie not to be so vocal with the pair, who would no doubt spread embellished gossip to the residents of the next hotel they decided to frequent. I was sure that many would be fascinated by the story of young Lord Garthorn and his romance with a servant. *Oh dear,* I thought. I would need to have a quiet work with Lottie — I wasn't aware of exactly how much she had divulged of her history.

As we continued along the boards, we reached stalls with colourful awnings flapping in the breeze, offering everything from freshly caught shellfish to candy floss. A small boy dashed past us with a red balloon which bobbed in the air behind him. Hamilton and I stopped to allow the others to catch up and we both leaned on the railings watching day trippers on the beach sitting in deckchairs.

"Such a beautiful day." I glanced up at Hamilton, who smiled down at me, his eyes crinkling at the corners.

"Positively!" the Major interjected. I hadn't noticed that our companions had caught us up. We followed them for the last stretch towards the main pier building. My dog's tail wagged furiously as he sniffed the air.

"I'm not sure we'll be able to take Prince inside the dance," I said. "He's too excited, with so much to see and sniff out here." My attention was caught by the sound of raised voices.

"You ruined your chances, you have no one else to blame but yourself!" Richard Sheringham had his wife by his side and was shouting at a man and pointed to him with his arm outstretched.

The man turned around, glowering.

"That's Herbert Lightfoot the dancer," I said to Hamilton.

Mr Lightfoot shouted: "I know what you did, I saw you and you'll regret it." He stormed down the boards towards us.

"I think we should take this opportunity to speak to him," I said.

"The man appears livid," Hamilton said.

I considered that as angry as Mr Lightfoot appeared, we did not have time to let suspects slip through our hands.

I called Lottie over. "We're going to speak to Mr Lightfoot." I gestured at the fellow, who was now much closer. "If you stick with the Simpson sisters and the Major, we'll find you afterwards. But let me have Prince," I said, holding my hand out for the leash. "I'm not quite sure we can take him inside and wish to seek permission."

Just as I was about to call out to Herbert Lightfoot, he stopped and retrieved a half-smoked cigarette from his pocket.

After Lottie had let go of the leash, she rubbed her arm as if she'd pulled a muscle. "I'll see you in a while." She trotted along the boards in order to catch up with the trio.

I stroked Prince and pulled one of his biscuits from my handbag. Again I spotted the letter I'd written, not really knowing why I carried it with me. "Here we are, boy," I said, placing a biscuit on the ground beside the railings. "Now behave yourself." I then leaned on the railings and looked to my right. "Oh, hello. It's Mr Lightfoot, isn't it?" I asked the fellow.

He turned around and frowned at me. "It is."

"Nasty business, isn't it?" I said. "Michel Blanc."

"Who are you?" he asked, narrowing his eyes.

"I'm Lady Ellen of Ashcombe Hall and this is…"

"Oh, yes. The great detective," he said in a sarcastic tone, and then looked back out to sea. "I hear the police caught the murderess." He took a long drag on his cigarette.

"We believe they have the wrong person in custody," Hamilton said.

Herbert stopped. "I hope you're not here to question me over it? I've heard of you. Read all about you. Anyway, I was at The Branden Arms all evening on Sunday."

"We came over to see the Sheringhams," I said. "You announced that you knew what they did. What were you referring to?"

"Look, I don't want any trouble. It was nothing to do with me." He took another drag on his shortening cigarette. "I was referring to Violet. She got too close to Michel."

"We hear that on Sunday, during the day, you had an argument with Michel on the promenade," I said.

"Ah, so little Eddie's stirring the pot, is he? I saw him staring at us." He paused then faced me. "It was the best job I'd ever had at The Grand." A faint smile appeared. "Dancing changed my life." Then his expression darkened. "But then Michel turned up and I lost everything." He looked away out to the waves. "I'm down on my luck and what you have to understand is that dance is everything to me. I feel less of a man without it and yes, I despised Michel Blanc, but I didn't kill the man." He shook his head. "Eddie's deflecting the attention from himself, because I'm an easy target, while he's dodging the bullet."

"You think Eddie had a motive?" Hamilton asked.

"He owed Micky a great deal. And now he won't have to pay him back a penny. Hopefully he'll be able to pay me back, though."

"Eddie owes you money?" I asked.

"He owes everyone. Look." He turned around to face me. "Eddie and Michel were often seen arguing. I always felt Eddie had something on Michel and I wondered if the money I saw pass hands was more like blackmail than a loan. Eddie lives at the hotel, he knows his way around, how to get to the ballroom and out again without being seen."

"That's interesting," Hamilton said.

"What about Richard Sheringham?" I asked. Whilst

Lightfoot appeared not to want to talk about his own issues with Michel, he surely was a good source of information on the other suspects.

"He's full of envy, with an angry streak. Which I've had to deal with a few times," Herbert replied.

"Why are you here, on the pier?" Hamilton asked.

"I asked for my job back. I'm stopping the drink. But Sheringham won't let me have another chance." He looked towards the pier building and I followed his gaze to see the Sheringhams still on the boards greeting customers. Lightfoot threw his cigarette butt into the sea. "Good luck with that pair."

"You said Richard Sheringham is full of envy. Did his wife give him cause to be jealous?" I asked.

"No, she's the sweetest women. Beautiful – it's not her fault she's admired. If he can't handle it he should have picked an ugly wife. He was always having a go at Michel, can't say I didn't enjoy it. I wanted Michel to cause problems, I wanted my jobs back. The one here and the one at The Grand." He straightened up. "I'm hoping Angus will give me a second chance, even if Sheringham won't. Once a period of respectful mourning has passed – of course!"

"Before you go," I said. "When you worked at The Grand, did you have any students called Rose?"

He frowned. "Over the years I'm sure I've had many students on holiday called Rose, but no regular person. No one local. The only Rose I know is the fortune teller at the fair, and she never comes anywhere near The Grand."

"Thank you for your help," I said and he strode away.

"There didn't seem to be much love between him and Michel," Hamilton said.

"The Frenchman was not a popular man." I glanced at the Sheringhams. "Now to tackle our next suspects."

CHAPTER 10

I wandered slowly down the pier with Prince and Hamilton by my side, and we soon approached Mr and Mrs Sheringham.

"Why is the fishmonger still here?" Violet said, gesturing down the boards to a shellfish stall.

"He has a lease. I can't evict him without reason, darling."

"There is a reason, it stinks! You know how upset I become at the smell of fish."

"Excuse me," I said as I approached them with a smile. "I'm Lady Ellen of Ashcombe Hall, and I do believe you are Mr and Mrs Sheringham, who own this delightful pier."

Richard frowned at me. "I've read about you in the newspapers."

"A lady?" Violet said, her indigo eyes wide open. The colour of them was quite mesmerising.

"And this is Captain Ernest Hamilton. We're out for a stroll with my dog."

Prince barked and sat beside me.

"We wanted to join the tea dance," I said. "I wonder, is there somewhere I can leave Prince, within sight?"

"Of course," Violet said, pushing her dark hair from her face as a gust of wind lifted it. "Follow me."

Her husband huffed as she led us away. I doubted I would extract any information from him, considering he clearly knew we had a reputation for being sleuths, but his wife appeared a lot more amiable. As we entered the pier building, we found Lottie, the Simpson sisters and the Major watching a juggler.

Lottie approached us.

"Mrs Sheringham is showing us where we can leave Prince whilst we attend the tea dance," I said.

"Oh, good." Lottie turned and called out to Betty, Nelly and the Major, gesturing for them to follow us.

After walking through the amusement building, we reached a large room at the far end. As we went inside, my stomach warmed remembering the times I'd been there with Papa.

We were met by a waiter. "Do you require a table?"

"Yes," Violet said to him, "and could you please open one of the doors, Lady Ellen's dog will sit there. And collect a bowl of water for him, too."

"Of course, Mrs Sheringham," he said with a nod.

Violet left the room before I could engage her in conversation. I followed the waiter as he opened a door and I tied Prince to a railing. "Now be good. We won't be long," I said as he settled down in what was thankfully a shaded area.

Back inside, the waiter led us all to a table not far from Prince. With the room having three walls made of glass, it offered a panoramic view of the sea and nearby Wales. The room was quiet, with only a few couples gliding gracefully across the wooden floor. I presumed with it being a sunny day, most had decided to remain outside and take advantage of what could be the last snatch of warm weather, considering we were now into September. The gentle sway of the dancers movements, combined with the backdrop of the sea, gave the illusion that we were aboard a cruise liner. As we took our seats, I remembered the afternoons of music I'd enjoyed there as a child, feeling exceptionally grown up.

Lottie settled beside me with Hamilton on my other. Opposite me was Major Fitzwilliam, as usual flanked by the Simpson sisters.

As the waiter handed us the menu, he inquired: "Would you care for tea or perhaps something more celebratory? We have champagne."

I glanced around the table, and it was clear from the expressions that met me that the others were in the mood for a treat. "Champagne all round," I said with a smile, determined to enjoy myself during this investigation. "And perhaps a pot of tea also and a selection of cakes?"

"Of course, my lady," the waiter responded, his smile broadening.

As he departed, we turned our attention to the dance floor. There were minimal traces of the modern world here, and whilst a little old fashioned, it had a comforting charm.

"It's beautiful, isn't it?" Betty said. "It reminds me of when I first met Luke."

"Ah," I said. "Who's Luke?"

Betty looked at her sister and then lowered her eyes, but not before I saw the sadness behind them. "The sweetheart of my youth."

"He passed away," Nelly added gently.

Betty looked up. "Like your husband, in the war, but…but we were never married."

"Which war?" I asked, wondering whether it was a later in life romance.

"The Boer," she said. "It was a horrid war."

"Devastating," the Major added as he smoothed his moustache.

"I too am aware of the pointless death war creates," Hamilton said. "It would appear nothing is learned, as I sadly witnessed atrocities in the most recent of wars." Hamilton looked downward and I glimpsed a flash in my memory of him at Ashcombe Hall, as a broken and dumb man. I was so proud of how he had pulled himself out of that gloomy and desperate state.

Betty smiled at me and I felt a pang of sadness, knowing how it felt to be widowed and parted from the one you love. There would never be a day that I did not think of, or miss, Leonard. I exchanged a look with Lottie who raised her eyebrows, then nodded at Betty and the Major. *It's never too late for love,* I thought, then glanced to Hamilton. *What's holding us back?*

"It's pleasant in here, isn't it?" Betty said, breaking the pause in conversation and no doubt attempting to lighten the suddenly sombre mood.

The Major nodded approvingly. "Tranquil," he murmured, then smiled at Betty.

The waiter returned, setting down a bottle of champagne and a pot of tea, along with an array of delicate teacups and saucers. He filled each glass with the bubbling liquid, as a waitress placed a tiered arrangement of food at the centre of the table. These consisted of scones with clotted cream and jam, delicate finger sandwiches, and an assortment of delicate cakes.

As we sipped our champagne, I found myself relaxing and the tension of recent days began to dissolve. I was brought out of the haze when the music shifted to a more upbeat tune and the doors of the room opened. A hush fell as the couples on the floor stepped to the side to allow Violet and Richard Sheringham centre spot. There was an air of anticipation as the owners came together in a hold, poised as if waiting for the appropriate place in the music before commencing their dance.

There was a collective sigh as they began to dance. Violet moved confidently, her long dress swirling as Richard led her around the room. She appeared different to when I'd seen her dance with Michel Blanc. Graceful and sophisticated. The Sheringhams were perfectly synchronised, as if they were the only two people in the room, and whilst there was an age difference between them, and I had originally considered them a curious pairing, in that moment, they appeared perfect together.

I leaned towards Lottie, whispering, "You would never know they were arguing just a half an hour ago."

Lottie nodded as she watched the couple. "They look so in love, don't they?"

As the dance came to an end, the room erupted in applause. Violet and Richard took a bow and curtsy before making their way around the room, speaking with those at each table. When they finally reached our table, Richard's demeanour changed somewhat. He squinted at me, clearly not trusting me at all.

"Are you here to spy on us?" he asked, his tone cold.

"Richard!" Violet said, as if shocked. "I'm so sorry, Lady Ellen. You are most welcome here."

Before I could respond, Richard grabbed Violet's hand and pulled her away, his forehead furrowed.

"Disrespectful," the Major said as he watched the couple move to the next table.

"I agree," Hamilton said, as Violet shot a nervous look over her shoulder at me and gave an apologetic smile.

"You're famous around here now," Betty said. "Everyone talks about you."

"Not everyone," Nelly said as if to reassure me. "Betty does tend to exaggerate."

"I feel as if I've outstayed my welcome in this town," I said with a sigh.

"Ellen, you're loved," Hamilton said, and the word *loved* dangled in the air like an endless echo in my mind.

I blushed. "Well, those who don't have much affection for me will be pleased that I've less than two weeks until I return to the hall."

"Do you think you'll catch the killer by then?" Betty asked, her eyes wide open.

I eyed the Sheringhams. "I'm going to try." I had to, for Mrs Flint's sake.

We continued to enjoy our cakes, although the atmosphere had been dampened by the encounter with Richard Sheringham.

"What do you think of them?" Betty asked, pointing to the door as the pier owners exited.

"Suspicious," the Major muttered, before downing the dregs of his champagne then reaching for another sandwich.

"I feel the same way," I said, wishing Mr Sheringham had been a little friendlier. I was still hopeful of being able to speak to Violet on the subject of Michel Blanc.

After another half hour had passed, I stood up. "Please excuse us, Prince has been left tied up for an hour. But you three do stay and enjoy the rest of the cakes. And it's my treat," I said, and placed enough money on the table to cover the cost and a handsome tip.

"Thank you, my lady," Nelly said with a smile that matched her sisters.

"We're most grateful," Betty said.

"Generous," the Major muttered with crumbs on his moustache as he eyed the remaining cakes.

I untied Prince and we left via a walkway which went around the periphery of the dance room. As we reached the main stretch of the pier, Violet approached us, as if she'd been waiting.

"Could I have a quiet word with you, my lady?" she said. "In private?"

"Of course, Mrs Sheringham. But might I bring Miss Penny with me?" I gestured at Lottie.

Violet hesitated for a moment, then nodded. "Yes, yes, that would be fine."

I handed Prince's leash to Hamilton. "Thank you." I gave him a smile.

He returned an encouraging nod. "I'll wait for you."

"Please, follow me," Violet said.

We returned to the pier building and walked through a side door just inside the entrance that led to a small office, tucked away from the public. It was a simple space, with a desk, a few chairs, and a window that overlooked the sea. Violet closed the door behind us, took a seat and folded her hands on the desk.

We sat down and it was quiet for a moment.

Lottie filled the awkward silence. "Have you always lived around here?"

"No, I came here after meeting Richard at the theatre in Bristol."

"Branden Bay is a lovely town," I said.

"Yes. Although it appeared much more sedate when

I first arrived. But there seems just as much crime as in the city. What with the untimely deaths of late, and I've had an item stolen myself."

"I'm sorry to hear that," I said.

She gave a dismissive wave of her hand. "Thieves are everywhere." She paused. "I wanted to sincerely apologise for Richard's behaviour." Her voice shook. "He's...under a lot of stress. He's had staffing issues this summer. There are many people around wanting jobs. but they're taking jobs that aren't suitable for them, or working here until they find something better, it's not been the best year for him."

"There's no need to apologise," I assured her. "He looked rather stressed Saturday evening."

"Ah yes, you were there. I recognise you now. You wore a green dress." Violet's face instantly became red. "I apologise for my behaviour. It was entirely my fault. Richard and I had argued. We have a...passionate relationship. And it's silly and childish of me, but I wanted to make him jealous. It was not what it looked like. My husband and I are deeply in love, no one or anything could ever come between us."

"When you danced with Michel, it looked to me as if you were well acquainted," I said.

"Of course I found Michel attractive," Violet said. "All women did, he was charismatic." She raised her eyebrows. "If my memory is correct, you too danced with him. The tango. I would say that sizzled compared to the dance I shared with him!"

I blushed remembering, and she certainly made a

valid point. I went on. "Did you ever speak to him on the subject of his past?"

"We sat occasionally at the bar together," she said. "He liked to talk about his life in the West End."

"Did he perform in London's West End before coming to Branden Bay?" I asked.

"Yes, and it's where he met the leader of the travelling music company. Most of his London performances were at the London Palladium."

"So you were friends with him, at least?" I asked.

"Of sorts. I may have confided in him myself…a little. Well…maybe more than a little. It was a mistake. It gave him the wrong impression."

"So whilst you considered him an acquaintance, he thought it was more?"

"Yes. I'm simply a warm person and I suppose people, or should I say men, sometimes think my genuine kindness is something else entirely."

Lottie sat, listening, allowing me to take the lead.

"And what about Herbert Lightfoot?" I asked.

"He taught me to dance before Michel came to town. He was ever so patient with me and taught me all the basic steps. But he began sending me flowers and that angered Richard. As you witnessed yourself, he's a jealous man. Herbert has piled on weight in recent months and the drink has not been kind to his complexion. Richard sacked him from the pier after I'd received an anonymous bouquet. Richard said that we could do the host dance ourselves here on the pier, considering how amazing a dancer I was, and he'd had lessons himself. Then..." She paused. "I hate to say it, but I complained about Herbert myself, to Angus Scott. I hope it wasn't totally my fault that he got the sack. I can understand why Herbert holds a grudge. I love dancing, it was always about the dancing for me, but Michel thought it was about him and I fear so did Herbert." She waved a hand dismissively. "All these men, it's rather tiresome, being deemed beautiful." She looked at me as if studying my face to decide whether I would also find this an issue.

"Where were you at nine-thirty Sunday evening?" I asked Violet, wanting to ascertain her alibi.

"At home with Richard. We ate supper and were in bed by eight."

Violet lifted a silver cigarette case and offered us one.

"No thank you," I said and watched her light a cigarette.

She exhaled a plume of menthol smoke. "I'd prefer it if you refrained from speaking to my husband, it will anger him."

"I'm simply tasked with clearing the name of Mrs Flint, the woman who has been arrested. To prove her innocence."

We bade Violet farewell and caught up with Hamilton who was with Prince, looking out to sea.

"Did you discover anything interesting?" he asked us.

"Violet said she never had an affair with Michel,"

Lottie said. "He got the wrong impression about them dancing together, that she loved dancing – not him."

"She told us not to speak to her husband," I added.

As we walked towards the promenade, we spotted Richard Sheringham marching up the boards towards us. He glowered and stopped. "I take it you're here poking your nose in about the death of the French dancer?" His eye twitched.

I had no intention of telling him I'd spoken to his wife. "Our friend has been arrested and is in the cells. She did not murder the man and we're simply trying to clear her name."

"It wasn't Violet. My wife is vulnerable. Michel took advantage of her kindness. Do not attempt to speak to her. We ate at seven on Sunday and she was with me into the late evening reading a book on our terrace."

Hmm, I thought, *that's not exactly what Violet said.* Someone was mistaken, or maybe both were lying.

CHAPTER 11

efore returning to the hotel, we'd given Prince a long run on the beach, throwing him sticks until he finally settled on the sand panting. I smiled at my dog. He was one of the only things that had been constant in my life over the past six years.

Once we returned to the hotel there was one person I was intent on speaking to – Eddie. Lottie took Prince up to our suite and Hamilton visited the reception to place a telephone call. As I entered the bar, Eddie was passing a drink to a customer. I waited until he was free and approached him.

"Could I speak to you for a moment?" I asked.

"Of course, my lady." He leaned on the beer pump, raising one eyebrow at me as he smiled.

"I understand that you owed Michel Blanc a sizeable sum of money?"

He straightened up as the smile slid from his face. "Who've you been talking to?"

"I was curious that you failed to mention it," I said.

He shrugged. "Why would I?"

"I understand you also have access to the ballroom via exits only known to staff."

"Every member of staff does." He gestured in the direction of the ballroom. "Who's been pointing the finger at me?"

"And I understand that you argued with Mr Blanc on a number of occasions."

"No, not really!" He regarded me for a long second. "I guess you've spoken to old Lightfoot." He turned away and picked up a cloth before wiping down the bar. "He knows where the access to the ballroom is as well. He lived in the staff quarters himself for years before he got the sack." He stopped. "Look, Herbert's obsessed with Violet. He hates that it was him who taught her to dance and then Michel whisked her away. She's got a spell over him. That's why he turned to drink. Not 'cause he lost his job, 'cause he can't get her out of his mind. He probably thinks I'm pointing the finger at him."

"Are you?" I asked.

"Yes, perhaps I am!"

"Where were you the evening of the murder?" I asked.

"It was my night off and I was in my room. I have no alibi." He shrugged. "But I don't need one. The police were happy with what I told them about that night. So unless you want a drink, I need to serve." His charm had completely fizzled out. Was he simply irritated by my questioning? Or did he have something to hide? I stepped aside to allow the next customer to order a drink and checked my wristwatch. The chef would no doubt be overseeing preparations for the evening meal. My next stop was to visit him. I decided to use the excuse of wanting some food to take to Mrs Flint. He knew her of course, as he'd worked at Millar's Hotel.

After asking a staff member for directions, I soon found the kitchen. It was huge compared to the one at Millar's Hotel, even though they had a similar number of guests.

"Lady Ellen," he said in his French accent when he saw me in the doorway. "You want to prepare some vegetables?"

I laughed. "Not today." I did so love to peel and cut vegetables – I found it calming and often did so at Ashcombe Hall. I had learned knife skills from a young age and also discovered that most of the village gossip was discussed in the kitchen. I had spent time with my cook as a child, after my mother had passed and continued to do so into adulthood. "I'm here to ask whether you have a meal fit for transportation, which I could purchase for Mrs Flint. I'm about to visit her."

"I heard that they have arrested her. I may have clashed a few times with her at Millar's Hotel, but she sticks to rules. She is a good woman and from what I hear, Inspector Stone – he is an imbecile."

I totally agreed with the chef. "Did you know the

deceased yourself?" I asked. "With him being a fellow countryman?"

"No. I called out to him and said how nice it was to have another from France at the hotel. He looked at me as if I was mad and turned away. He was an extremely rude man. I am sad that he has been killed, but not surprised. If you cause trouble, you pay the consequences. As we say in France: 'He who sows the wind, reaps the storm.'" He called out to one of the cooks. "Could you please prepare a ploughman's meal with cheddar and cold meats. And add fruit." He turned back to me. "I will have it ready in half an hour and will send it to your room. Do send my regards to Mrs Flint. She's a strong woman, remind her of that."

I thanked the chef and returned to my suite. Hopefully Mr Flint had been to visit his wife. Ina was in need of all the support she could muster.

THE POLICE STATION was not far but the chef had been most generous with food for Mrs Flint, and Angus Scott had insisted on the hotel covering the cost and that I should be chauffeured by the hotel motorcar. I took the steps up to the police station door, which the chauffeur opened for me, and luckily Inspector Stone was not in sight. I was shown to Mrs Flint's cell by PC Jones.

Mrs Flint burst into tears as soon as she saw me. "I feel like I've been abandoned."

"I've been doing all I can," I said, placing the box on

the bench and sitting beside her. "Has your husband been in yet?"

She shook her head. "Poor Douglas is so upset about this. He can't face coming here, he's not even leaving the house." She pulled a handkerchief from the sleeve of her dress and wiped her eyes. "Thanks for seeing him, I really appreciate it and I'm sure he does too. He sent me a letter." She pointed to a sheet of paper at the end of the bench. "He's so hurt by this. He said the Inspector was adamant that I'd committed the murder. I feel so ashamed that I sloped off like that, not telling Douglas. And it was stupid, now I look guilty. I wish I'd never had the lesson." She wiped her nose. "Douglas said he'll come in, he just needs time to forgive my lies, and I don't blame him."

I had less sympathy for the man. "You've done absolutely nothing to be ashamed of. You're an innocent woman who had plausible reasons for not telling your husband about the dance lesson. And how were you to know that someone was going to kill Michel and that you would require an alibi?" I reached for the box I had brought. "Now, take a breath. I've brought some delicious food from Chef Moreau who sends his regards. He has faith in your innocence. He said it's clear that you are a good person and to remind you that you are a strong woman."

Mrs Flint sniffed. "That's very kind of him."

"You need your strength. So eat as much as possible, and the fruit will keep fresh for a few days."

"I hope I'm out before it goes rotten," she said.

I sat for a while as Mrs Flint ate the food.

"Do you know yet who did it?" she asked me.

"I have a few suspects." I brought her up to date.

"So the best bet we have is to find the woman I saw. The one called Rose, who's from London. I'm so grateful, my lady, for you taking the time to help me. Even if I end up taking the blame and..."

"Don't speak like that, Ina, we will ensure you're released. And in the event of a hearing, I'll appoint the best solicitor that money can buy."

I FELT SOMEWHAT DEFLATED as I took the downhill stroll to the promenade. As grateful as Mrs Flint was, I had no idea who had killed Michel Blanc. As I turned the corner of Beach Road, I stopped and squinted. Ahead of me was a man who resembled Mr Flint heading into The Branden Arms. I quickened my step and once I reached the public bar, I stepped inside. The place was thick with smoke which stung my eyes. It was busy, with much laughter from the predominantly male clientele. I could not see Mr Flint but spotted Mrs Kerr, the landlady. I had met her when dealing with a previous case. She was pulling a pint and laughing. I wondered what age she was. She had dark hair but she may have coloured it to keep the grey away. I deduced that she was probably in her late thirties. I'd discovered during an earlier case that she was a widow, having originally run the pub with her late husband.

"There you are, old Pete." Mrs Kerr handed a beer jug to a grey-haired man who had few teeth.

"Hello Mrs Kerr," I said as I approached the bar. "I hope you're well."

"Wouldn't have expected you to come in here," she said with her eyebrows raised. "Especially alone."

"I've visited Ina Flint and thought I saw her husband come in here. I wanted to have a short talk with him but can't see him." I took another glance around the room.

She frowned and also looked around. "Oh? I haven't noticed him." She ran a hand through her hair, then leaned over the bar and lowered her voice. "I heard about Ina. I can't believe that she was carrying on with the Frenchman and then killed him." She sighed. "Takes all sorts, I guess."

"I can assure you that Mrs Flint is innocent." I looked about me, but Mr Flint was still nowhere to be seen. *Maybe I was mistaken,* I thought. He had been some distance from me along the road. "She needs all the support she can get."

"If you say so, my lady." She sniffed. "Now, what can I get you?"

"Oh, nothing for me thank you."

"Be sure to pop by with your gentleman friend." She raised her eyebrows and gave a small smile. "The captain."

I felt my face heat up. *Do people think we're a couple?* I wondered to myself. "Good day, Mrs Kerr," I said and promptly left without further comment.

As I headed back to the hotel, I considered my reaction to Mrs Kerr's assumption that Hamilton and I were courting. *Why was I so defensive?* I thought, when it was my wish that we become closer. I realised with reluctance that as much as I said that the expectations of society did not bother me, they clearly did. I pushed those thoughts away, as I did not like the way they sat with me and wondered how on earth I was to search London for a woman called Rose. It appeared that Inspector Stone's enquiries were currently concerned with proving Mrs Flint to be a murderer, and I wondered whether he would even bother to consider that line of enquiry. There was a slim chance that Rose was staying at The Grand Hotel, as she had asked Michel to return to London and it was late. She was unlikely to have travelled back to London that evening, assuming she had travelled there by train.

Once I reached the hotel, I spotted Angus Scott walking around the reception seemingly inspecting it for cleanliness.

He looked up. "Lady Ellen, how are you?"

"I'm in good health, Mr Scott, and am able to update you." We sat in a pair of plush upholstered chairs situated in the bar. After explaining to him my progress, he agreed that we needed to check the hotel records for any guests called Rose. At the reception desk, he requested the guest register then led me and the receptionist to his office.

"Gloria was on duty that evening." He gestured at the staff member.

"I was, yes." She smiled at me.

"We're looking for a lady called Rose – however, we are not aware of her surname," I said.

"Rose," Gloria said as she ran a finger down the register. "There's a Mrs Rose Timmis. She was here with her husband George Timmis and their son." She looked at me. "She was about forty-five."

"This woman is around thirty according to Mrs Flint's description," I said. "She had brown hair, tied back, and wore a blue coat.

"There was a woman that evening of that description. She wasn't a guest, but I told the police about her already," Gloria said.

"What about her?" Angus boomed, sitting to attention.

The receptionist put a hand to her chest, probably as a reaction to Angus's loud voice. "She asked me where the ballroom was, so I asked if she had a lesson booked with Michel as otherwise it was closed. She said no, but that she had some business with him."

"You didn't mention this before?" Angus said.

"You told us not to discuss the matter, sir." She visibly gulped. "And I already told the police."

"You're not in any trouble," I said, raising my eyebrows as I regarded Angus, whose face was extremely red.

"No, no, of course not," he said.

Gloria continued: "I said to the police that the woman was clearly mad." She lowered her voice. "Michel did often attract odd women. I guess that's what happens when you're too good looking. That was what killed him, I'm sure." She pulled a handkerchief from her jacket pocket. "I had quite a soft spot for him. I'll miss his daily *bonjour*."

"Why did you think the woman mad?" I asked.

She gave a short laugh. "She said she was his wife!"

"His wife?" Angus boomed again.

This is indeed a valuable piece of information, I thought, and gave a sigh of relief. I had something to work on.

"I wonder if the police are following this up," Angus said. He turned to Gloria. "Where did the woman go after that?"

"She clearly wasn't his wife. She had a London accent and was very ordinary looking. But the telephone rang, so I had to take the call, and when I was finished with it, she'd gone. Although Mr Lightfoot was here, and I had him to deal with."

"Herbert Lightfoot was here the night Michel died?" I asked.

"Yes, although I didn't get to mention that to the police as when I was talking to them, Ina Flint came in and well, the Inspector spotted her and after a very brief conversation, he arrested her."

"How was Mr Lightfoot that evening?" I asked.

"Drunk." She shook her head. "He often is." She glanced at Angus as if not sure whether to continue.

"Go on," I said.

"He was still complaining about losing his job and

asked if Eddie was serving. I told him no, it was Eddie's night off and he left."

"Why was it exactly you sacked Mr Lightfoot?" I asked Angus, to ensure I had the correct facts.

"We'd had a few complaints, as Gloria said, the man likes to drink excessively and he's become much worse. It was the right thing to do, you can't have a dance host staggering around on the ballroom breathing fumes all over the guests. I'd had to send him to his room numerous times." He paused. "And now I feel a little responsible. If I'd not given Michel Blanc the dance host job, the poor man might still be alive."

There followed a short silence of contemplation.

I turned to Gloria. "Did you see the woman proclaiming to be Michel's wife again?" I asked.

"She certainly wasn't a guest here and no, I've not seen her since."

"Thank you, this is most useful information," I said.

"I'm sorry if I should have spoken sooner," she said. "I told the police, so I presumed…"

"You've done nothing wrong," Angus confirmed.

Once the receptionist left the room, I turned to Angus. "The police have information about the wife, so I hope they're following it up."

"But what if they're not and there's a killer on the loose? What will Dora think when she returns?"

"As the killer is not Mrs Flint, I'm afraid the killer is indeed at large. However, Mrs Flint said that Rose told Michel he must return to London, so I presume that is where she is."

I left Angus's office and spotted Hamilton, looking extremely dashing as he stood next to a large potted fern in reception. *Oh no*, I thought. I'd totally forgotten the time and that I was supposed to at that point be dressed for an early dinner, for we were due at the cinema.

"I'm so sorry, Ernest," I said as I reached him. "Events have moved on and I was completely lost in the case."

He smiled down at me. "Ellen, it's fine, I'm pleased to see you. I was worried and not sure whether to visit the police station."

"I need to dress for dinner. You must be hungry. But I have much to tell you. And I must make notes." I checked my wristwatch. "Let's order food to my suite and ask Lottie to make a note of my findings, and then we can go to the cinema."

"So THE ROSE woman was actually his wife?" Lottie said eagerly as she wrote in the notebook.

"The receptionist was convinced the woman was mad, as Michel had made no mention of being married and she considered the woman too plain to be married to such an attractive man."

Hamilton tutted. "Was he really that attractive?" He frowned at me.

I hid a small smile. "I think it was more the way he presented and carried himself. Take away his suit, the tidy moustache, the perfectly slicked hair, the charm and French accent."

"And that look on his face," Lottie said, gazing into the distance. "The half smile with one eyebrow raised like he loved himself."

"And yes," I continued. "He would otherwise have had rather ordinary looks."

"Even though he looked really dashing," Lottie said.

Hamilton huffed. "So you think it's feasible that he had a wife and she was this plain woman called Rose?"

"It's the only thing we have to go on. And if she's his wife, we now know that we are searching for a Rose Blanc in London. Which makes tracing the woman much easier."

"Of course," Hamilton said. "Do you think the police are following this line of enquiry?"

"I've no idea what Inspector Stone is doing," I said. "And I've no intention of asking him. But the woman was likely to have been staying in Branden Bay on Sunday evening as there was no late train."

"So we can go around all the hotels and guest houses asking if they had a Rose Blanc staying," Lottie said wide-eyed.

"I could look for her in London," Hamilton said. "I'm catching the nine o'clock train tomorrow."

"Won't you be too busy at your meeting to look for her?" I asked.

Hamilton stared at me for a thoughtful moment. "You could come with me, Ellen?"

A fizzle covered my body as I looked into his blue eyes.

"Yes," Lottie said. "We could all go to London. Sebastian's there, he could help too."

"We can't take Prince to London," I said with a shake of my head. "He needs space to run in." As if understanding, my poor dog lifted his head, and gave a sorrowful whine.

"Ellen, I would be honoured to accompany you." Hamilton looked to Lottie expectantly.

Lottie exhaled so completely that her body appeared to deflate. "Yes, of course, I'll stay and look after Prince," she said in a small voice.

"Are you sure?" I asked with a flutter of excitement which had nothing to do with the prospect of finding Rose Blanc.

CHAPTER 12

*I*t was with much excitement that I boarded the train to London with Hamilton. We had cancelled our trip to the cinema the previous evening, and in its place had an early night. Amongst the passengers were a few weary holidaymakers returning home. The morning train was not crowded, unlike the late train often filled with tired and sandy day trippers, although those would now be fewer, as the temperature had dropped. However, if the train had been busy, we would not have been disturbed as Hamilton had organised a private compartment and insisted on paying. He was a gentleman through and through.

The train creaked out of the station, as we left an extremely drizzly Branden Bay. Lottie waved at us from the platform with Prince sitting beside her. I knew she wished she was coming with us. That morning whilst eating an early breakfast, I'd agreed to take her letters for Sebastian with me and drop them to him at his parents' Mayfair home. I dreaded the prospect of seeing his mother, who had been less than pleasant towards me the last time we'd met. I had felt even more guilty at leaving Lottie behind, when she'd explained how she missed her family. I had clean forgotten that they were also in residence at the Band-berrys' London property and had letters and a gift for them. As Lottie had wept, I'd toyed with the idea of sending her to London with Hamilton instead, but quickly dismissed that. I was after all on a mission to locate a possible murderer to ensure Mrs Flint's release from police custody. I'd asked the Simpson sisters to keep a keen eye on Lottie and after a debrief with them and the Major, they had eagerly agreed to visit every place of lodgings in Branden Bay with Lottie, to ask if there had been a Rose Blanc in recent residence.

"It's ridiculous, isn't it?" I said to Hamilton. "That we have a seventeen-year-old young woman and three older people scouring Branden Bay for details of where Rose Blanc lodged the night of Michel's death, whilst the police continue to blame Mrs Flint."

"Lottie seems much brighter this morning. I did feel rather guilty leaving her behind," Hamilton said.

"I've brought her letters to pass to Sebastian and I agreed to invite him to travel back with us."

"I see," Hamilton said as if he did not approve.

"I try not to encourage the relationship, but she's so completely in love and he does appear to be genuine with his attention. It's not unheard of, for people to marry outside of their class. After the war and everything I've witnessed, the whole class system seems irrelevant and it doesn't bring happiness – look at me!"

"Ellen," he said with concern in his eyes.

"Oh, sorry," I said. "I'm not looking for sympathy. And I'm happy. It's simply that those things that matter most, health and the love of one's family, are not guaranteed. When death comes knocking it matters not what money you have. Maybe hard labour strengthens the body?" I smiled at Hamilton. "But now, I'm living more for the day and today, I feel extremely happy."

He held my gaze and I felt the common connection between us. I turned as the door to the compartment opened.

"Tickets please," the guard said. He checked them. "Thank you, my lady." I could tell by his accent that he was local to the South West of England and it appeared he'd recognised me. I was finding it a little disconcerting being recognised by strangers outside of Ashcombe. At least I would be anonymous once we reached London.

"What's our plan of action?" Hamilton asked.

"I think the best route to finding Rose Blanc will be to visit the London Palladium to ask if anyone remembers a Michel Blanc and his wife Rose, and hope that someone will know which parish he lived in."

"We could check the electoral roll," Hamilton said.

"I'm not sure if he would be listed, considering he was French."

"If he'd married an English woman and had been

through a process of naturalisation, he may have," Hamilton said.

"His accent was strong but his English was pretty good," I said. "So he could have been here for a while, especially if he spent some years at the Palladium. Yes, that's a great idea."

I removed the notebook from my bag and smiled as I saw Lottie's handwriting. As much as I relished the idea of a couple of days spent with Hamilton, I was already missing her and Prince. I suddenly realised there had not been a day I'd spent without my dog since he came into my life. But I knew he was in good hands.

The first two hours of our journey flew by. Luckily, we'd managed to book the express train with fewer stops. Hamilton read his newspaper.

"Ah, there's an article about Michel Blanc here, with a picture of the chap," Hamilton said. "This will be useful during our enquiries." He folded and then ripped the paper, extracting the article for me.

I placed it in my bag, again noticing my letter to Hamilton. *I should have left that at the hotel,* I thought. I retrieved a book I'd bought. I'd had little time to read fiction whilst away from the hall, but was enthralled by 'Greenmantle', John Buchan's follow up to 'The Thirty-Nine Steps'. I was deep into the narrative and jumped as the guard opened the door again.

"Just to inform you, my lady, that your reservation in the restaurant car has become available."

I looked at Hamilton.

"I made the reservation," he said. "In case it was busy."

"How thoughtful," I said and put my book down as the guard left the compartment.

Hamilton and I stepped from our compartment and the door closed with a soft thud. The corridor was narrow with mahogany walls. I steadied myself as the train swayed. The wheels squeaked as we took a slight bend. As we neared the restaurant car, I heard the muffled voices of fellow travellers which became louder as Hamilton slid open the heavy door. Inside the dining car, the tables were set with white linens, silver cutlery, and porcelain plates bearing the name of the GWR railway company. We were seated and the glasses swayed with the motion of the train. I touched mine, worrying it would fall. A waiter approached holding a menu card embossed with gold lettering.

"Thank you," I said and then checked the meal on offer which was cream of asparagus soup, with a saddle of lamb for main and a peach melba for dessert. Having read it I felt famished.

"What time is your meeting, Ernest?" I asked once we had confirmed we were happy with the menu.

"Three o'clock this afternoon."

"I'm planning to visit the Bandberrys in Mayfair. I'm rather hoping that Sebastian is at home and his mother is absent. No doubt she has been inviting many young women to take luncheon, afternoon tea and dinner with him."

Hamilton gave a short laugh. "I can imagine. Will you be welcomed by them?"

"It's unlikely, but I wish to pass Lottie's letters to Sebastian personally, so will ask the butler to inform him of my arrival and hopefully he will not alert Lady Bandberry. I find her snobbery towards me tiresome. If I'd been born a male, I would now possess the title of the Earl of Ashcombe. Instead with no male heir in the dwindling family, I inherited the estate with no title. It fills me with sadness that my forefathers' legacy has ended abruptly, simply because I'm female. This is why I wish to preserve Ashcombe Hall as the home it was." The hall was undergoing renovations following its time as a convalescent home.

"Your soup," the waiter said as we leaned back so that he could place the bowls before us. We began to eat our food in silence.

We retired to our compartment after the tasty meal and read for the remainder of the journey. I felt completely comfortable in Hamilton's presence, with the silence being far from awkward as he read his newspaper and I read my novel.

The train whistled as we pulled into Paddington Station. Once we had disembarked, Hamilton hailed a taxicab and he took us to the Savoy, on a route which passed Buckingham Palace.

As the taxicab pulled into Savoy Court and up to the hotel, I felt a flutter of excitement. This was indeed the most modern of hotels in the entire country. I understood that it had been built to include all the modern expectations of American guests to entice them to visit London. Indeed, Mr and Mrs Millar of Millar's Hotel in Branden Bay had modelled their much smaller hotel on the Savoy. I opened my bag to locate payment for the car and hesitated, spotting the letter I'd written for Hamilton. I felt a blush creep over my face, wondering if I would be able to broach the subject of the future before we returned to Branden Bay. Or whether I should simply hand him the letter. I had hesitated for so long that Hamilton had paid the driver and was already out of the taxicab and opening the door for me. He offered me his hand with a reassuring smile. I grasped it and carefully stepped out of the motorcar. The city sounds were muted here, as the hotel entrance was slightly set back from The Strand.

The doorman tipped his hat as we passed through the grand doors and into the reception which had marble floors and chandeliers. We were met by the scent of oriental lilies, which were arranged in vases upon the reception desk, where a clerk smiled at us. We checked in separately.

Hamilton left for his meeting which was only a short walk away, after leaving his bag with the porter. I entered my room and was not disappointed. It was beautifully decorated. I then thought back to Ina Flint and reminded myself that I was in London with a purpose. I decided to wash and change my dress for my trip to Mayfair.

. . .

AN HOUR LATER, as I stepped out of the taxicab onto Upper Grosvenor Street, I admired the row of elegant townhouses. The London residence of the Marquis and Marchioness of Bandberry had a grand entrance, however I slipped down the narrow alleyway running alongside the house, which was just wide enough for a delivery cart. Around the back, hidden from view of the street, I found the tradesman's entrance. I rapped on it and hesitated for a moment, listening for footsteps on the other side, but there were none. After a second knock with no response, I reached for the handle and turned it, pushing the door open to reveal a dimly lit passage. I glanced around, noticing the smell of food cooking. My footsteps echoed as I walked along the stone floor until I entered the kitchen. It reminded me of my own back at Ashcombe Hall, with a large oak table dominating the space around which were staff who all stopped speaking when they noticed me. I instantly guessed that the young woman kneading bread was Lottie's sister. They looked so alike and I was hit with a stab of emotion. *Poor Lottie*, I thought, considering she had been separated from her family when she was banished from the house due to her friendship with Sebastian.

"Can I help you?" a woman dressed in cook's attire asked.

"I'm Lady Ellen of Ashcombe Hall," I said.

The young woman kneading bread stopped and her jaw dropped. "Lady Ellen, who employs our Lottie?"

"Indeed, and you must be her sister, for there is a likeness."

The young woman stood and bobbed a curtsy. "I am, my lady."

"I'm Lottie's mother," the cook said. "But whatever are you doing in the kitchens?"

I handed over the parcel I'd been carrying. "Lottie asked me to pass you a gift of fudge and she has also written letters."

"That's most kind," Mrs Penny said. "I'm surprised they let you down here."

"Actually, I let myself in the tradesman entrance." I gave a small smile.

"Oh, my goodness," Mrs Penny said. "But before you leave, my lady, I want to say how thankful we are for you employing our Lottie. After what happened here with the young lord."

"Is Sebastian at home?" I asked.

"Who wishes to know?"

I turned around to find myself faced with the Bandberrys' butler.

"Good afternoon, Peterson," I said, his name coming to me in a flash as I looked at his face, even though it had been some years since we had last met. "Could you please let Lord Garthorn know that Lady Ellen is here to see him?"

"In the kitchen?" he growled.

I gave a short laugh. "Ideally, yes."

The man huffed but walked away.

"Don't worry," a young man said, dressed in a

formal black tailcoat, striped trousers, a white shirt, and a waistcoat. I assumed he was the under butler. "The Bandberrys are out. Lord Garthorn's here alone."

Sebastian soon entered the kitchen. "Ellen, what a surprise! Come this way and we can talk."

"Would you like me to arrange refreshments, Lord Garthorn?" Mrs Penny asked.

"That would be kind," he said to her with a fondness one would not usually expect to see in a London house such as this between a resident and their servant.

I bade my farewell to Lottie's family and followed Sebastian up the stairs to the Bandberry drawing room, which was just as I remembered it, opulent with many family portraits.

"What brings you to town?" he asked. "Is Lottie well?"

"Yes, she is. I accompanied Ernest, he has a meeting concerning his Cairo trip and we're in the midst of a new murder investigation." I explained to him what had happened to Michel Blanc and it was clear that Lottie's letters to him had indeed been intercepted, as he knew nothing of the strangling at all. I ended with: "I'm staying at the Savoy whilst we attempt to trace Rose Blanc."

"Is Lottie with you?" he asked.

"She's had to remain in Branden Bay with Prince, but I've letters for you from her." I opened my handbag and retrieved them. "She's posted a few but by your surprise at hearing of Michel Blanc's death, I'm assuming they've not reached you."

He shook his head. "Mama has intercepted them, no doubt! If I have to endure another introduction to a young lady my mother considers a suitable future bride, I may very well go mad." He took the letters from me. "I miss Lottie desperately. When are you returning to Branden Bay?"

"We have booked the four o'clock train tomorrow afternoon."

"Could I possibly accompany you when you return?"

"That would be super." At least I had accomplished one of my goals so far. I knew Lottie would be delighted.

"Let's leave before my parents return home, which I imagine will be rather soon as they met Lord and Lady Gillingham for luncheon." He gave me a rue smile. "They have a daughter."

As we left the house, I realised that the potentially romantic meal I had planned with Hamilton would probably include an additional guest.

CHAPTER 13

J had left Sebastian in the American Bar at the Savoy whilst I checked my appearance in my room. I was about to leave when the telephone rang.

"Lady Ellen," I said as I answered.

"I have Captain Ernest Hamilton on the line. Go ahead."

"Ellen, I've returned from my meeting. Did you visit Mayfair?"

"I did, and Sebastian is waiting for me in the American Bar," I said.

"Oh." The disappointment in his voice was evident.

"How was your meeting?" I asked in a cheery voice.

"I sail in seven days."

I was pleased that he was telling me this over the telephone so that I did not have to force a smile. "How long does the journey to Cairo take?" I asked.

"It depends on the weather conditions and the

number of ports visited on the way, but I should be at the port of Said within two weeks and then we stay for as long as it takes to arrange onward travel via rail."

It seemed even worse, being that far from Hamilton, knowing that if I wrote to him, it would take at least two weeks, more likely three or four before he received my letter. *So far away,* I thought. And would there be an address I could send it to? Considering he was on the move most of the time.

He must have sensed my reaction due to my pause as his voice brightened. "I'm here at the hotel in my room, I'll meet you in the American Bar."

As I replaced the telephone mouthpiece into its cradle, the feeling that I needed to tell Hamilton how I felt about him was overwhelming. Thoughts and pictures of me waving him off at Branden Bay railway station came to mind, and were akin to the memories I held of waving Leo off on Ashcombe Village platform for the last time. I realised that it was my failure to tell Leonard that I loved him more than anything in the entire world before he left that had affected me. I gulped; the thought that I had not told him that I would love him for an eternity still crushed me, over six years later. I'd just assumed he would know. But had he known? *Why is this becoming worse now?* I asked myself. *What's wrong with me?* I moved a stray hair from my forehead trying to collect myself, wishing I'd brought Lottie and Prince with me. I realised what a support they both were. As I checked my reflection, I forced a smile and eradicated the sorrowful thoughts, then picked up my handbag and went to the door.

Downstairs, I entered the American bar. It was elegant and modern. I had frequented the bar before and the cocktails were wonderful – various concoctions, mixed by American barmen who made the most delightful recommendations. I spotted Sebastian, who was seated and reading a book. The young man was rarely without one. As I approached, he rose from his chair and waited for me to sit down.

"Ernest will be joining us shortly," I said. "He's setting sail in seven days."

His face brightened. "In that case, we must speed up this investigation."

I heard Hamilton's voice behind me. "True, I can't leave the country not knowing what happened to Michel Blanc."

"Ernest, pleased to see you," Sebastian said, rising from his chair to shake his hand. "What's our next move?" Sebastian asked as Hamilton sat down.

"I think we should leave the strong martinis until later," I said. "It's rather amusing, isn't it? To be sipping American cocktails, whilst across the Atlantic, they've banned the very thing they invented."

"It somehow makes cocktails feel delightfully rebellious," Sebastian said with a laugh.

"So where shall we begin our hunt?" Sebastian asked.

"We'll be visiting the theatres," I said. "Starting with the London Palladium to ask if anyone knew Michel Blanc and then if we do find someone that remembers him, to locate his wife's residence."

Having had light drinks rather than the strongest of cocktails the American Bar had to offer, we hailed a cab and headed for the Palladium.

As the taxicab slowed to a halt outside the theatre, I caught my breath, watching the lights that spelled out 'The Midnight Follies' above the entrance. The rain had only just stopped, and the wet street reflected the lights. I stepped out of the taxicab with Hamilton and Sebastian and we entered the foyer, which was quiet as the performance was in progress.

"This is a good time," I said. "We can question the kiosk staff."

"I'm afraid it's started," the doorman said. He nodded at Sebastian. "Lord Garthorn." I took it that Sebastian was a frequent visitor.

"We're here sightseeing, really," I said. "A dear friend of mine has passed away and we're frequenting places he performed."

"I'm sorry to hear of your loss," he muttered.

"I don't suppose you've heard of a Michel Blanc?" Hamilton asked the man.

"Nah, never heard of her."

"Not Michelle, Michel – he was a French entertainer," I said

"No, and I've been here for years. No French that I

remember." He gestured at the kiosk. "But you could ask Enid, to make sure."

A woman smoking a cigarette with a lined face studied us as we approached. "You're too late."

"We're not here for the performance," I said. "I wonder, do you remember a French performer here called Michel Blanc?" It was then that I remembered I had the newspaper article and removed it from my bag. It was folded with the picture of Michel visible. I handed it over.

She squinted at the page as if focussing in on the face.

"I believe he was from northern France," I said.

"Nah, from south..." She put her hand to her mouth as she coughed.

"The south of France?" I asked.

"Where, exactly," Sebastian asked eagerly. "Nice? Marseille?"

She began to laugh and coughed again. "Nah, South London. He's from Lambeth not France." She continued to laugh as she unfolded the page to reveal the headline of the article stating *Body Found in Ballroom*. The smile slid from her face and she stubbed her cigarette out in an already full ashtray. "Poor old thing."

"You knew him well?" I asked.

"Yeah, but he ain't French. He's as English as me, lived in Lambeth. And his name, it ain't Michelle or whatever you said, it's Micky. Micky White."

"Of course," I said. It made sense now, the fact that he didn't respond to me when I spoke French to him, and ignored the chef – he clearly spoke little to no French at all and had no wish to be exposed.

"You knew him well?" Hamilton asked.

"Not as well as many who worked here, mostly women."

The doorman also joined us, out of curiosity. "Did you say Mick is dead?"

"I'm afraid so," Hamilton said. "We're looking for his family. With the police believing he was a Frenchman, they're looking in entirely the wrong places, so his poor wife may not know."

"Poor Rose," Enid said.

"It was bound to happen one day," the doorman said. "He liked to live dangerously that one. I take it, it weren't no accident?"

"No," Sebastian said. "He was strangled."

"I said he'd go after the wrong woman one day. Did he die at the hands of a jealous husband?" Enid said.

"We don't know, but we wanted to pay our respects to his wife," Hamilton said.

"Poor thing, at least she won't have to worry about him no more," Enid said.

"Do you know where I could find her?" I asked.

"Not sure of the address but I know she goes to church. Opposite the palace?"

"Buckingham?" I asked with a frown as there was no church opposite the King's residence.

"No, Lambeth, where the Archbishop lives." Enid shook her head as she took a sip of her hot drink. "As sad as I am, he probably got his comeuppance. He went for any woman he fancied, no matter whether they were betrothed or not. I mean, while I was here, there was Ethel, Ruth..."

"And Sarah, and not forgetting poor Phyllis," the doorman said.

Hamilton gave his head a slow shake. "So, his wife is called Rose White?"

"Yep." The woman lit another cigarette. "He was a good dancer. I loved him in Rockets."

"Ah yes, I adored that show too," Sebastian said. "Excellent comedic moments."

Enid laughed. "He was great as that French painter weren't he?" she said to the doorman, then paused. "Guess that's where he got the idea from, to pretend he was French!"

"I heard he went south west," the doorman said.

"Yeah, Eddie told us he spotted him when he was home on his break."

"Eddie?" I asked.

"Yeah, young lad. He couldn't wait to get away from here once he was old enough. Was brought up in a workhouse he was. Now he's got himself a job at a big hotel in some seaside place near Bristol."

It was then I remembered that Eddie had once referred to Michel as Micky – the young man had some answering to do!

AFTER A LATE MEAL which the Savoy were good enough to serve us, we returned to the American Bar.

"Tomorrow, we shall visit the church and see if we can locate Rose White," I said. "But until then, I'm in need of a mental break."

"Father says the dry martinis here are the best in the country," Sebastian said as he enjoyed one.

"Apparently, it's all down to the proportions of vermouth and gin," I said. "Leonard loved a dry martini." I looked over my wide rimmed glass at Hamilton, who now appeared thoughtful. Was it my mention of Leo? I could not ask, considering we had Sebastian with us, and now I felt as if the tables had been turned and that Sebastian was our chaperone.

"I can't wait to return to Branden Bay," Sebastian said. "It's so nice to be free of the shackles of my parents and their expectations of me. It's always been that way, the pressure. I know it sounds disrespectful and ungrateful, but sometimes I wish I'd had an older brother, one who would appreciate all the pomp and tradition."

"You've always felt that way?" I asked.

"Yes, even when we were children. I used to wish I could swap places with Lottie, she always seemed so happy and carefree compared to me." He paused. "I ran away once. I was upset as we were at the country house and Lottie had remained in London. I was playing in the grounds, throwing sticks into the river from the bridge, then wondered where the road led and kept walking."

"How long were you gone for?" I asked.

"A week. And it was one of the best weeks of my

life. I reached the mining town of Radstock. By this time I'd been on the road for a couple of days and was dirty and famished. I stood outside a bakery and gazed at the lovely warm bread. The owner came out and offered me some bread and dripping. She took me in and I told her I'd run away, that I'd fallen out with my parents."

"I take it you didn't tell her who you're your parents were?" Hamilton said.

Sebastian laughed. "No. She had two younger boys. She said they couldn't learn and she would love them to find job in one of the cities when they were grown so they could leave Radstock, as the only options were mining or working in the family bakery. I taught them their alphabet and how to write their names and they began to read after only a few days. Both were extremely bright, they simply hadn't had the correct teaching. They told me their master at school was evil. I told the mother and she asked if I would stay on and teach them whilst I worked part time in the bakery. I felt for the first time in my life that I was doing something worthwhile. That I belonged in a family, a real family."

"Is that where you discovered your passion for teaching?" Hamilton asked.

"Yes, as soon as I returned to Bandberry I taught Lottie to read and write. It made me feel needed."

"So did you just decide to go home?" I asked.

"No, Peterson was visiting a cousin and spotted me. The family were so fearful, they thought they were going to be accused of abduction! Eventually, Papa sent them some money as a thank you for caring for me once I'd spoken to him."

"So, you told your parents you were unhappy?" I asked.

"My father said once I matured, things would change, and that he understood they were putting pressure on me, and that it was Mama's fault for only giving him one child. I was not punished, they were simply relieved I was home. They had already brought Lottie and her family over, not because of me, but because Mama prefers Mrs Penny's cooking. But I never forgot that week and what it felt like to be part of the world instead of above it."

As I watched Sebastian go on to speak of his hopes and dreams, I knew deep in my heart that he would never let Lottie down intentionally – and I also saw a part of myself, the part rebelling against my own obligations.

CHAPTER 14

The following morning, Hamilton and I shared an exquisite breakfast together and afterwards, Sebastian met us in the foyer. He'd convinced his family chauffeur to take us to Lambeth. We settled into the plush motorcar. Hamilton sat beside me, his gaze fixed frontwards, whilst Sebastian, ever fascinated by the world around him, leaned forward, chatting with the driver about the changing face of the motor industry. I remained quiet as we passed a clattering omnibus. So many people, were caught up in the everyday rush of a September week-day, their coats flapping behind them. London always seemed to move at twice the speed of the rest of the country.

We continued along the Strand, passing the windows of shops and cafés. Big Ben's clock face loomed ahead and marked the hour as we crossed Westminster Bridge over the Thames.

On the other side of the bridge, the view of Lambeth Palace came into focus, its red-brick a contrast to the stone of the Houses of Parliament on the opposite bank. As we approached the church of St Mary-at-Lambeth, the motorcar slowed to a stop outside. I opened the door and Sebastian helped me out. The church was much larger than any of those in the south west I had frequented.

"If the Archbishop is in residence, we may not be permitted to ask questions," Hamilton said.

I gestured towards the church. "Let's go inside, I'd like to see the interior at least."

As we entered, my heart beat faster as I saw the back of a woman seated before the altar. She wore a navy coat with her brown hair tied back. She turned at the sound of our footsteps and I knew instinctively that this was Rose White.

"Stay here," I whispered to Hamilton and Sebastian, and walked towards her.

"I've been waiting for you," Rose said in a shaky voice as we met half way along the aisle, her eyes red. "News travels at speed in this town. I know you visited the Palladium and were looking for me. And that Micky…" She trailed off then broke down.

Without thinking on the matter, I automatically returned to myself as a nurse, greeting the wives who visited Ashcombe Hall to pick up their husbands' belongings after they had passed. I hadn't lost many men, but some had come to us when there was no hope for them.

"I'm a widow myself, and I know nothing I can say will ease your pain in this moment. All I can do is sympathise with you and let you know that this level of pain will pass." I looked at the altar. "And you have your faith."

She swallowed and took a deep breath. "I have to power on for the children."

I felt stunned. I'd not considered at all that Michel, also known as Micky, was a father. "I'm so sorry, I didn't realise."

She gestured to the exit of the church. "Oh, don't worry about the kids, they hardly knew their father. Even when he lived here, they never saw him. He was at the Palladium most of the time." She paused. "And often stayed out all night. I'm sure you already know what sort of man he was? But it don't mean I didn't love him. Do they need me to confirm his identity or something?" she asked.

I needed to tread carefully. "The police are still making enquiries," I added tactfully.

"So who are you?" she asked. "I guessed you were friends with Micky?" She crossed her arms. "Were you and he...?"

"No!" I said, which echoed slightly and I realised I had spoken too loudly as a woman tutted from a pew in the front row. "I'm friends with the woman the police are holding in the cells."

"You're friends with the killer?" Rose's voice echoed around the church, bouncing off the flagstones.

The praying woman turned and frowned at us.

"Sorry Bertha," Rose whispered, then motioned for me to follow her. As we reached Hamilton and Sebastian, they joined us.

Once outside, we stood under the cover of the entrance as it was again raining.

"The arrested woman did not kill your husband," I said. "We want to discover who did."

"We would appreciate it if you could help with our enquiries," Hamilton said.

"You're investigators? Coming in here pretending to care about me? Who do you think you are?" She gestured at Hamilton. "Sherlock blooming Holmes?"

"I think we should find somewhere else to talk," I said as the chaplain gave us a stern look from just inside the door.

"I ain't going nowhere with you," she said.

"Mrs White," Sebastian said. "We really do need your help. We have to find who really killed your husband otherwise they may kill again."

"You don't think they'll come after me, do you?" Rose said. "Why did they kill him anyway?"

"We don't know that. But it would help us if you could come to Branden Bay. After all, your husband will need to be laid to rest," Hamilton said.

"I ain't bringing him back here," she said.

"We can arrange a burial in Branden Bay," I said.

"I can't afford it," she said defiantly. "He'll have to have a pauper's grave. He was sending me money every month. Then it stopped." She wiped her nose. "But I'll need the death certificate."

"If you don't come with us," Hamilton said in a patient voice, "the police will likely collect you."

"Why will they collect me?" she asked with a frown.

"You were one of the last people to see your husband alive," I said.

Her jaw dropped and her eyes widened. Then she shot a nervous glance at Hamilton. It was then that I realised she had no idea that we knew she'd been spotted in Branden Bay.

Rose opened her mouth and then closed it. "I take it Eddie told you!"

"No," I said, "he didn't." And I was intending to find out why the barman failed to mention that he'd also seen Rose in Branden Bay, as well as failing to inform anyone that he knew Micky from London and that he was not French! "You told the receptionist you wished to see Michel Blanc and that you were his wife."

"Oh yes, I clean forgot," she said with a gulp. "I didn't give my name. But I never knew he was dead. I was out on the first train Monday morning."

"Has Eddie not sent news about your husband's death?" I asked.

She shook her head. "Maybe he's written..."

"Were you aware that your husband was masquerading as a Frenchman?" Hamilton asked.

"Yes. He told me a few weeks ago, when he actually came home to visit us. He said he earned more money being Michel. But after that visit, he stopped sending anything. That's why I went to see him."

As we left the church grounds, Rose promised us

she would meet us at Paddington Station at half past three. We had offered to cover the rail costs. I felt rather satisfied that we'd achieved our aim of finding the victim's wife, but felt none the wiser as to who had actually strangled him.

THE COMPARTMENT FELT a lot different on the return journey with the four of us. Rose was now extremely quiet. I guessed the reason was that as soon as we'd boarded the train, I formally introduced everyone. She became quiet after discovering that Sebastian was the son of the Marquis and Marchioness of Bandberry. Due to their links to the royal family, they were a lot better known than others of the aristocracy. It was in those moments of acknowledging Sebastian's level in society that I feared most for Lottie. No matter how much the young man loved her, it appeared impossible to think he would one day marry a previous servant of the family.

I pulled my book out of my bag and placed it beside me.

"Ah, Greenmantle," Sebastian said. "How are you finding it?"

"It's such a gripping tale," I said. "I love the espionage and intrigue. Buchan paints the most vivid picture of secret missions. I can hardly put it down."

"I read it in one sitting," Sebastian said. "Stayed awake all night. He truly knows how to create suspense."

"We're booked into the dining car at six," Hamilton said as he picked up his newspaper.

"Oh, I er…" Rose began.

"Don't worry, my dear. The meal is covered," Hamilton said.

"I've not travelled first class before," Rose said, looking around the compartment and rubbing her hand on the upholstery beside her.

Now engaged in conversation, I decided that as I had her undivided attention, I would ask her some questions before I passed the matter to Sergeant Chambers.

"We know that you were in the ballroom with your husband before he died and that you said he must return to London, otherwise he would no longer exist."

She frowned. "No, I didn't mean that he wouldn't exist, I meant I would expose him as being from South London, not France! It's Michel Blanc that wouldn't exist any more – not Micky!"

"Ah, that makes perfect sense," Hamilton said, smiling at her. He always wished for women to be innocent; I on the other hand was not so convinced.

Rose smiled at Hamilton. Having realised he was not of the upper classes, he now appeared to be her preferred person in the compartment.

"And where did you go when you left The Grand?" I asked.

"I stood in the reception for a while," she said, "catching my breath. I found it upsetting and had to wipe my eyes. A woman came over and asked if I was okay."

"What did she look like?" I asked.

"Dark hair. Friendly face. A bit older than me I'd say."

"And her name?" Sebastian asked.

"She didn't actually say. She asked me what the matter was. I guess I looked upset. So I told her, my husband was always unfaithful and was in Branden Bay pretending to be French, and I'd caught him with another woman."

"When did you catch him with another woman?" I asked.

"That night in the ballroom. I walked in there and they were together. Their faces only inches apart."

"Were they dancing a tango?" Sebastian asked. "I noticed he got rather close to his partners on the dance floor." He shot me a look and I felt my cheeks burn; Hamilton noticed and frowned. My dance with Michel Blanc was something I wished to put to the back of my mind.

"It was no tango," Rose said. "I said to him 'How dare you? Have you no respect?' Well the woman turned around." She gulped. "She was so beautiful. Darkest hair I've ever seen and deep blue eyes, like sapphires they were. I'd never be able to compete with a woman like that! She pointed at me and said, 'Who are you?' And before I could answer, Micky said 'my wife,' in his fake French accent. And do you know what she did? She laughed, didn't she! Then the smile was wiped off her face when she realised Micky weren't joking. She shouted and cursed at him. Well, she was carrying herself like a proper lady with a posh frock and jewels, but the words that came out of her mouth you'd expect to hear at Billingsgate from the fish wives. Then she looked me up and down and said. 'You can keep him,' and stormed off!"

"And what was her name?" I asked, even though she had described Violet Sheringham perfectly.

"That's what I asked him. 'Who's she?' and he said 'no one.' He told me he was working on getting enough money so he could come back to us and we could move somewhere nice, and neither of us would have to work again."

"What was he doing to raise the funds?" Hamilton asked.

"Oh, I didn't believe him. I'm sure he was just stringing me along. Then some other woman came in. Older, about forty I'd say. He put on his fake accent again and said he would be right with her, then pushed me towards the door when she had her back turned. I felt as if he was throwing me out! That's when I told him to come back to London or else. He called after me but that was the last time I saw him." She lowered her head and looked at her hands.

"How stressful for you, Mrs White," Hamilton said gently.

She sniffed. "It is, and now I've gotta go through all of this and explain myself to the police. I wish I'd never found out. I would've been happier thinking he'd run away rather than him being dead."

"Eddie would have told you in the end," I said. "But I can help with your alibi," I said, thinking this would be an excellent opportunity to ask her further questions.

"You can?" she said.

"Yes, you simply need to explain your movements." I took out my notebook with haste, and the letter I had written Hamilton fell out of my handbag. I stared at it as it tumbled as if in slow motion to Hamilton's feet. "I'll get it," I said quickly as he began to move forward. I swiftly retrieved it, hoping that he had not noticed to whom it was addressed. I returned it to my bag as my cheeks burned, avoiding Hamilton's gaze.

I moved the hair from my now hot forehead. "Sebastian, could you make notes?" I passed him the notebook and my pen. "So," I said. "When did you see Eddie?"

"Outside the hotel, he was going inside and spotted me. We didn't talk for long, I just said that I was there to have a word with my husband." She sighed. "I could tell as I looked in his eyes that he felt sorry for me. I think he was embarrassed as he made a quick excuse and hurried away."

"Could you please go through what happened after you left the ballroom? You said that you met a dark-haired woman in the reception and then what happened?" I asked.

"She comforted me and suggested we go to a bar she knew where they had music to cheer me up."

"And what was the bar called?" Sebastian asked.

"It was a man's name?"

"Jake's?" I asked.

"Yes that's it, Jake's Jazz Bar. Well, she was all nice, asked me all about it. What Micky had got up to. I really bent her ear, but I think I went overboard and spoiled her evening, 'cause she said she was going to powder her nose and then disappeared. I ended up walking back to my lodgings all on my own."

"Where were you staying, and did anyone see you at your lodgings when you returned?" I asked.

"Kinklaven guest house and no, the door was on the latch and I went to my room."

"Is there anything else you can tell us about the woman?" Sebastian asked. "Her eye colour?"

"Brown. She didn't have anything odd about her appearance."

"Hopefully we can ask Jake to confirm you were there and find out who this woman is. I wasn't convinced Rose had a solid alibi.

"So how did you meet your husband?" I asked.

"We were up at the Palladium together. He was handsome when he was young. Even more so. We fell in love and got married. Real quick." She looked down at her belly. "And had the twins. Well, it was expensive, so he started working longer hours taking on more shows and acts in the Palladium. I guess he started to find me boring. He went with other women. It's been tough."

Hamilton passed her a fresh handkerchief. "I'm sure

you've done an amazing job bringing your children up alone."

"I've had help from Bruno. Micky's brother. He's always been sweet on me. I think we'll probably get together," she said in a matter-of-fact way.

"I know this is hard, but can you think of anyone who would kill him?" I asked.

"Well, I don't want to speak ill of the dead, but Micky once blackmailed a man. He might have been up to no good again. Micky was no angel."

"I think it's time for our supper," Hamilton said.

"I need to, er, fix my make-up," Rose said, even though she wasn't wearing any. I gave her directions for the onboard lavatory.

After she had left the compartment, Hamilton turned to us. "I don't understand what women see in these men who have nothing to offer."

I smiled at him. "It is not just a man's wealth that makes him attractive."

He looked at me intently.

I felt momentarily held within his gaze. I knew I had to speak to Hamilton before he sailed. What if he were to meet a lady overseas? He could strike up a romance not realising that I had feelings for him. I had to say something as time was running out – but this was not that moment.

WHEN WE ARRIVED at The Grand Hotel, Angus was in reception to meet us.

"Lady Ellen, was it a successful trip?" he asked me, then regarded Rose.

I turned and beckoned Rose to my side. "This is Michel's widow," I said. "His real name was actually Michael White – known as Micky. His French name and persona were in fact part of his act."

"He wasn't French?" Angus asked.

"No," I said. "And I wondered whether you have a room available for Mrs White at all? She will be visiting the police station tomorrow morning, but will need a decent sleep before then." I did not say, but I was worried that Inspector Stone might order for her to be incarcerated at the police station. So I considered she would require a decent meal and sleep before enduring that ordeal.

"Of course," Angus said. "I have the key to Michel's room if you'd like to take a look tomorrow." He softened his voice and focussed on Rose, "There may be some items you wish to keep."

"Thank you, Mr Scott," she said in a quiet voice.

"Lord Garthorn will be staying in my room," Hamilton said. "I have an extra bed. We will of course pay an additional fee."

I accompanied Rose to the room Angus had arranged for her to ensure she was settled in, and then arranged to meet both her and Angus after breakfast in the reception at nine o'clock.

CHAPTER 15

When I reached my suite, Sebastian was waiting outside. He clearly realised it would be inappropriate for him to enter without me. Once inside, Prince barked frantically, and Lottie squealed.

"I've only been away for one night," I said with a laugh, realising that Lottie was squealing at Sebastian who had followed me in. I turned away and stroked Prince, leaving the pair to embrace. I did not want to witness anything I should really disapprove of.

"You missed me then?" Sebastian said to Lottie,

"All I've been doing is sitting here writing piles of letters for you."

"I read three on the train," he said with a laugh.

"Let's sit down," I said. "I've ordered supper to the room and Ernest will be here soon. We can update each other."

Hamilton was soon in our room, looking as if he'd

shaved. I too had taken time to freshen up and felt a little more awake. I'd styled my hair into place with a little pomade and changed my dress. I felt so much better since we'd returned to Branden Bay and I put that down to Lottie. My world simply felt brighter with her in it, and I was so pleased that she'd agreed to return to Ashcombe with me.

We brought Lottie up to date as she sat wide-eyed, and Sebastian passed her the notebook which now had been completed in all three of our hands.

"That explains it then," she said. "Yesterday at Kinklaven guest house, the owner said that a woman stayed there with Rose's description but that her name was Mrs White. She didn't even know her first name. Just wait until I tell the sisters he was English – now we know why Eddie said Michel was a fraud." She opened her eyes. "What on earth will the Major say?"

"Blighter," Sebastian said, mocking Fitzwilliam and pretending to stroke a huge moustache.

Even Hamilton grinned and he was not one for mockery. As we laughed together, I felt so at home with them that I near wept at the thought of us being parted.

Lottie composed herself, giving one last giggle before speaking. "Norma and Mr Breckon are back in town after their trip to Minehead. I went up there today with Prince to visit them."

"Did they get the positions they applied for?" Hamilton asked.

"The hotel owner said they'd let them know." She

poised over the notebook. "What's the plan for tomorrow?" she asked me.

"After breakfast, I'm visiting Michel's, I mean Micky's, old room with Angus Scott and Rose. I will then escort Rose to the police station and whilst there, visit Mrs Flint. After that, I wish to focus on two of our suspects who have been less than honest with us. Firstly, Eddie, who knew exactly who Micky was and secondly, Violet, who failed to mention that she was one of the last people to see Micky alive. I feel we need to gather more information before we can come to any conclusion."

"I'm sure you'll get to the bottom of it, Ellen," Hamilton said.

Lottie closed the notebook and placed it on the coffee table.

"The night is young," Sebastian said. "Maybe we should go to Jake's Jazz bar to check Rose's alibi. I'm feeling awake."

"That's a great idea," Lottie said.

"I agree," Hamilton said with a smile.

"Will you be good?" I asked Prince.

"I'll arrange for a maid to sit with him," Lottie said.

A WHILE LATER, I arrived at the reception with Lottie to find Sebastian and Hamilton chatting to Betty.

"I hear you're off out," she said. "I've just convinced the captain here to have one drink with us before you leave." She slid her arm into Hamilton's and gazed up at him.

He forced a smile at her. "A small one."

Lottie, Sebastian and myself followed them to the bar area of the ballroom where Nelly and Fitzwilliam were seated.

I heard Hamilton huff as he sat down, even though the band played at quite a volume.

"Good to see you back," Nelly said. "And you, Lord Garthorn." She smiled at Sebastian and then turned back to me. "Was it a successful trip?"

I took my seat and placed my bag on my lap. "I'll leave Lottie and Sebastian to let you know." I turned to Hamilton and smiled as Lottie chattered away to them. I was just about to speak when I noticed a tall man dance by.

"Oh, look," I said to Hamilton. "It's Herbert Light-foot, looking a lot smarter than we've seen him before." I was quite astonished. He wore new clothes, and without the ill-fitting suit he did not look quite so over-weight. His hair had been cut and his face clean shaven, apart from his moustache. But more than anything, it was the elated expression upon his face. He looked quite handsome compared to the slovenly man I'd spoken to on the pier and seen slouched over the ballroom bar.

Hamilton raised his eyebrows as Lightfoot whisked a young giggling woman around the dance floor. "He appears to have tidied himself up somewhat, I hardly recognised the chap."

"Angus must have given him his job back," I said.

After the dance had concluded, Herbert strode past us on his way to the bar.

"Mr Lightfoot," Hamilton said. "Congratulations on regaining your position."

Lightfoot stood tall. "I've been given a second chance, and I won't let Mr Scott down."

A woman approached him. "My husband has twisted his ankle, could you give me a dance?"

"I'd be delighted." His face lit up as he led the woman to the dance floor. I was struck by how the man had come alive.

We were soon sipping drinks that the Major had bought us, although I noticed that Hamilton was drinking his rather fast, no doubt hoping to escape the hotel sooner, rather than later.

"I saw you speaking to Mr Lightfoot," Betty said. "What a change in the man."

"That's not surprising," Nelly said. "He has his livelihood back."

"And his loan written off," Betty said.

"What loan?" I asked.

"He owed Michel money," Nelly said. "Or should I say Micky."

"How do you know that?" I asked.

Betty exchanged a glance with her sister and then over to where Eddie was shaking a cocktail. "Eddie tells us all sorts when he's had a few drinks."

"His tongue is loose," Nelly said with a nod.

"He told us that Michel was a fraud, married and an adulterer," Betty said.

"When did he tell you that?" I asked.

"Yesterday evening," Nelly added. "Lottie has updated us to say that his wife is now staying at this hotel?"

I nodded. "She's going to the police station tomorrow."

"Did she do it?" Betty asked wide-eyed. "Do you think they'll release your friend?"

"Apparently Mr Michael White was unfaithful multiple times," Hamilton said with a shake of his head.

"For years, by the sounds of it," Lottie added.

"Maybe he got what he deserved," Nelly said, then pursed her lips. "It's a shame if his wife takes the blame, though. Lottie said she has children?"

"She has no motive," I said. "He was still supporting her and the family financially, and now she has nothing. Although she told us that he stopped sending funds recently, which is why she visited him here in Branden Bay."

"She's a sweet God-fearing woman," Hamilton said. "Not the type to strangle a chap. She's a dainty thing."

"I need to speak to Eddie, too," I said, glancing at the bar. He appeared to be keeping a lot of information back and I wanted to know why.

"Eddie won't have done it." Betty put a hand to her chest. "He's a good boy."

It appeared to me that Eddie had charmed the

Simpson sisters, but I wasn't as convinced that he was as innocent a young man as they suggested.

"It's a confusing world," I said with a sigh.

"Death," Fitzwilliam said.

Hamilton frowned. "I beg your pardon?"

"Everywhere," the Major said.

Betty tapped his hand. "Wally gets upset about the war, don't you dear?"

"Pointless," he said. "Too many lives stolen."

"He lost a lot of friends," Betty said in a soothing voice.

I looked to Hamilton, whose head was tilted to one side as if lost in thought.

"And I lost my love," Betty said with a hiccup and glassy eyes.

"Aw, Betty." Lottie put her arm around her.

I saw in Betty's eyes a look of loss that I recognised, then glanced at Fitzwilliam's sorrowful expression. I really hoped these lost souls could come together. However, I was concerned when I turned and saw how strained Hamilton's face appeared.

"Shall we make our way to Jake's?" I said.

Hamilton's face broke into a smile. "Yes, let's."

I stood up. "It's time for us to brave the nightlife." I smiled at Lottie and Sebastian. "I do not wish to leave it too late."

ONCE OUTSIDE I SHIVERED, realising I'd forgotten to pick up a coat.

"Here," Hamilton said as he removed his jacket and then placed it over my shoulders. It felt warm and had the scent of his cologne. We followed Lottie and Sebastian, who were arm in arm for the short walk to Jake's.

As we stepped into the jazz bar, we were met by the chatter of the crowd and the music, which always lifted my mood. The atmosphere was completely different to the ballroom at The Grand. In comparison, it seemed alive as if it had its own personality. Jake approached us through the smoky haze; it was as if the place was an extension of him.

"Lady Ellen, so pleased to see you back." Jake, as always, managed to find us a table near the back, away from the crowd but close enough to view the band.

Once we'd ordered our drinks, I sat back and took in the music. I was always impressed by the way jazz was like a conversation between the clarinet, the piano and the double bass, each player appearing to follow their own rhythm and melody, yet still keeping to the beat of the drum. Exploring their own space, yet still together in the same key which appeared to change from time to time. Whilst they often played the same pieces of popular music, it felt different each time. As I listened, I felt the tension of that endless day, which had begun at the Savoy, melt away.

Hamilton and I watched Lottie and Sebastian dance. It was far too modern for either of us to confidently join the young couple on the floor.

"My life is going to be so dramatically different at the end of next week," I said to Hamilton. "I'm not sure how the staff will receive me. I feel quite changed. Changed by the war and now changed even further. I feel…" I trailed off.

Hamilton stopped and looked at me over the candlelight. "Like a commoner?"

I laughed. "That was not the word I was searching for, but in a way, yes. I've felt free. As much as I'm blessed with so much, I feel tied to the hall. The feeling of going back." I gulped. "It's overwhelming." I stopped, worried my emotions would run away with me, and it was not fair to foist them upon Hamilton. A man who'd witnessed atrocity first hand. It felt insensitive to complain when I was in a most fortunate position.

I was interrupted by Jake. "Would you like another drink?"

"No thank you, as soon as my young friends have finished their dance, we will retire for the evening. It's been a long day," I said. "However, I do have a question concerning last Sunday evening. Do you happen to remember two women arriving at about nine o'clock? Both with dark hair?" As I said it, I realised how ridiculous it sounded. I laughed before he had a chance to reply. "I'm guessing you see hundreds of people."

He nodded. "I do indeed."

Lottie and Sebastian returned.

"And now, we must leave," I said.

As we commenced the short journey back to the hotel, Hamilton remained silent but reached for my hand. I pretended we too were courting, like the young couples walking alongside us, and tears stung my eyes, for I knew I only had days left with him. We turned onto the main Beach Road and were still holding hands as we passed The Branden Arms when the door burst open. Hamilton pulled me into his arms to protect me. I looked up, so close to his face, with my heart thumping.

"Oh, it's you two," a man said.

I looked to my side to find Douglas Flint in the public bar entrance.

"I wouldn't have thought smooching in a dark doorway was the type of thing someone of your sort would do," he said, then descended into laughter.

Hamilton released me. "That is not what is occurring here, I can assure you."

"I seen it with me own two eyes." Flint laughed again and went inside the pub.

Lottie and Sebastian had caught us up and I looked at the now closed door. My face felt hot. "Let's go and speak to the man," I said. Mr Flint had angered me, not so much for his rude behaviour, but because he had interrupted my moment with Hamilton. "I wish to enquire whether he's been to the cells to visit his poor wife."

"Are you sure?" Hamilton asked.

"Are we all going in?" Lottie asked.

"Absolutely," I said, not wanting to leave the pair alone.

Hamilton opened the door and we went inside. The pub was extremely busy and the final orders bell rang. Hamilton jostled his way across the room, making a pathway for us. Mrs Kerr threw her head back from behind the bar and laughed with a customer, her dark hair shining under the dim light.

"Mrs Kerr," I said when we reached the bar, which was crowded with those keen to order their last drink. "I'm looking for Mr Flint."

"I can't see him," she said.

"Where is he?" Hamilton demanded. "We saw the man come in here!"

She pursed her lips.

"I want to speak to him about his wife. It's important," I said.

Mrs Kerr passed a pint of beer to her regular customer. "There you go, Old Pete." She placed a hand on her hip and narrowed her eyes at me. "That woman has hurt Doug. You might think she's innocent, but she's broken his heart. Carrying on like that."

"I've no wish to discuss the Flints' marriage with you," I said. "I simply wish to speak to the fellow."

"You'll have to wait here," Mrs Kerr huffed and walked away.

"I've seen a new side to that woman," Hamilton said. The last time we'd interacted with her, she'd discovered a dead body on her property. A local gangster used to rent space from her to run his business. She seemed quite compassionate at the time, seeing through his faults to care about the fellow. Now I was wondering whether Mrs Kerr lived life connected to the crime world herself.

Mr Flint appeared from a door at the end of the bar. "What do you want?"

"Mr Flint!" Hamilton began, I knew he was going to berate the man for not addressing me in a polite fashion.

"It's fine, Ernest," I said then turned back to Mr Flint. "I wondered how Ina is?"

"I've not seen her." He crossed his arms. "I'll wait for her to be released, seeing as you're so convinced she's innocent." He gestured around the pub. "Everyone around here thinks she done it. And they know her a lot better than you do!"

"Show some support, man," Hamilton said.

"I think you should worry about your own kind. Now if you'll excuse me, my *lady* and *captain*." He gave a sarcastic bow and walked away back through the door he'd entered from.

"Well, I never, the rudeness of the man," Hamilton said.

"What do you think he's doing back there?" Lottie asked.

I looked over to the other side of the pub where Mrs Kerr was now talking to Herbert Lightfoot, who must have finished work. He was laughing and joking with her.

"Such a change in the man," I said to Hamilton.

"It's to be expected. His life has improved since his rival was murdered," he said.

I turned around to see Lottie and Sebastian slipping through the door that Douglas Flint had taken. "Oh, my goodness," I said. "Lottie and Sebastian have followed Mr Flint."

"I'll get them," Hamilton said, then stopped in his tracks as the customer Mrs Kerr had referred to as 'Old Pete' stood in our way.

"So they won't let you play then?" the elderly gentleman said.

"I beg your pardon?" I asked him.

He gave me a toothless grin. "Roulette. They won't let me play neither. They only let Sheringham in 'cause they know they can fleece him." He cackled. "It's rigged." He tapped the side of his nose.

"I see," I said. "And is Douglas Flint allowed to play?" I asked.

"Allowed? It's him what runs it."

I looked over the old man's shoulder to see Lottie and Sebastian returning to the bar.

"That's enough, Old Pete," Mrs Kerr said as she joined us. She gestured at Lottie and Sebastian. "Where have you pair been?" she asked. "That's private property!"

"You appear to be running a gambling house," Sebastian said.

Lottie looked at him wide-eyed as she bit her lip, then stared at Mrs Kerr, waiting for her response.

A flash of concern covered Mrs Kerr's face. "There's no harm in it. I got to make ends meet, since Crow was done in. I found that table with his stuff, he must have bought it from a casino. It's a harmless bit of fun and a nice little earner for me. I need the men here, in case there's trouble. It's not easy being a woman in business on my own. And don't you judge me. You've no idea about normal folk."

"Look here, Mrs Kerr," Hamilton said. "Lady Ellen is an extremely compassionate woman and all that concerns her is protecting her friend, Mrs Ina Flint."

"Richard Sheringham gambles here does he?" I asked as Old Pete slipped away.

"Yes, and I can give him an alibi for the dancer's death if you want it," Mrs Kerr said. "He was here Sunday evening; as the bars shut early, I lock them in. It's a private gathering. So you can't go blaming the dancer's death on him. he was here."

"What about Mr Flint," I said. "Was he here?"

"I, er. Well, no. He was at home. Obviously. Now, if that's all that concerns you, it's time for you to leave." She about-turned and we followed her to the exit. She thrust the door open, emphasising that we had outstayed our welcome.

Lottie and Sebastian walked ahead of us, eagerly discussing the case.

"It's been an immensely long day," I said to Hamilton.

He took my hand and smiled at me.

I faced front as a smile also covered my face. "But not an entirely unpleasant one, as I've spent it with you."

"I cannot complain," he said.

He squeezed my hand and did not let go until we

had reached the landing of the third floor of The Grand.

He paused. "Good night, Ellen."

I smiled and gave him a kiss on the cheek. "Good night, Ernest."

I walked to my suite with Lottie beside me, still with a smile upon my face.

"I had a lovely evening, Ellen. It was so exciting, thank you so much for bringing Sebastian back."

"He didn't require any persuasion," I said with a laugh as Prince bounded up to us.

The maid startled awake from the chair and stood up. "My lady."

"I'm sorry, we were much later than we planned." I reached into my pocket and gave her a few extra coins."

She stared at her palm. "Are you sure, my lady?"

"Of course, and now you must retire otherwise you will yawn your way through tomorrow."

She curtsied and left the room. It was a reminder of how I was treated in Ashcombe. When I'd arrived in Branden Bay, it was my wish to forgo the airs and graces and to be treated like anyone else, and I certainly had experienced that from people such as Douglas Flint and Mrs Kerr!

"I'm looking forward to going to Ashcombe, but it's going to be sad saying goodbye to the people of this town," Lottie said. "Like Norma, John and even Mrs Flint. I never thought I'd grow to like her. And I love the Simpson sisters. Betty was nearly in tears telling me how much she's fond of me." She paused. "I love Betty, she reminds me of Mum."

I smiled. "There is a likeness. Your mother and sister love you very much, that was clear when I met them."

"I wish we could take Betty and Nelly back to Ashcombe."

I laughed. "I think they would soon become bored."

Lottie began to cry. "I miss my family and they seem like family to me."

I leaned over and gave her a hug. "As soon as we settle, I promise to take you to visit your family. Betty would simply be a substitute; I will ensure you do not lose touch with your kin."

"Thank you, Ellen."

As I went to my separate bedroom within the suite, I glanced out of the window and opened it to let in the fresh air, listening to the sound of the moonlit waves. I eased onto the bed with the window still open and lay there for some time, finding that now overtired, I could not sleep.

Later, I heard cries. I sat up, not knowing what to do, realising it was Hamilton enduring a night terror. *Poor Ernest*, I thought. It was probably the earlier talk of war with Major Fitzwilliam in the ballroom. I had an overwhelming urge to go to his room, but instead rolled over, listening until the cries stopped, knowing Hamilton had been woken, probably by Sebastian.

CHAPTER 16

We ate a delicious, cooked breakfast in the morning. I made no mention to Hamilton of hearing his night terror, and Sebastian certainly did not mention it. I would not have expected him to either. He was chatting away to Hamilton in a breezy voice. He was an admirable young man and I hoped that when he inherited the title of Marquis of Bandberry, he would remain the man he was during the summer of 1924.

The Simpson sisters sat with Major Fitzwilliam, looking over his shoulders as he read his newspaper.

Nelly looked up. "The Vigilante Slasher's been at it again."

My heart skipped a beat. "Where?"

"In London," Betty replied.

"When?" Lottie asked.

"Two nights ago."

"The victim was far from innocent!" Hamilton said,

clearly having already read the piece in his own newspaper.

"That's true," Nelly said. "It says here that the man abused many in a workhouse which lead to deaths. He escaped charges and the gallows."

"He must have been guilty if the Slasher got him," Betty said.

"At least it's in London and not here," Lottie said, rubbing her arm.

"What time exactly did he strike?" I asked, my mouth dry.

"In the early hours," Nelly said. "As the man slept."

"And he took the fellow's necklace," Betty said. "He wore a gold chain with a shark's tooth on it."

"The Slasher has quite a collection of trophies by the sounds of it," Sebastian said.

"Yes, we heard he has a pipe, a woollen hat and he took a lock of hair, too," Lottie said.

"He does better than the police," Betty said.

"I for one do not condone the Slasher's attacks," I said. "If he was simply doing it to help the police, he would stay undercover and not leave a rather gruesome calling card of slashing their inner arm. It speaks of a man not well in the mind."

"Agreed," Fitzwilliam said.

"Maybe he wants to highlight the inadequacy of the police," Hamilton said.

"I fear the man simply seeks significance and notoriety," I said in a somewhat haughty tone. "He's far from philanthropic."

"You have a point, Ellen," Sebastian said.

"I said it before, and I'll say it again," Lottie said. "He just likes killing and picks on rotten people so he don't feel so bad about it."

"We'll never know what drives the man," Hamilton said. "I can't see the fellow ever being caught."

AFTER BREAKFAST, I reached the reception at nine o'clock and was relieved to find Rose White standing by one of the large potted ferns speaking to someone. As I moved around the pot, I hesitated. Eddie had placed a hand upon her shoulder. He looked up and seeing me, hurried away. I was overdue a long conversation with that young man. Rose turned and gave me a nervous smile.

"Good morning," I said. "You were speaking to Eddie?"

He was offering me his condolences." She took a deep breath. "I'm feeling a little nervous about the day ahead. It all seems so real, now I'm here at the hotel."

"I'll take you to Angus's office," I said in a gentle voice, realising it was better to expedite the search of Micky's room.

Angus rose from the chair behind his desk as we arrived in his office, to which the door was already open. "Morning, my lady and Mrs White." He lifted a key from his desk.

"I understand there's a route to the ballroom via the

staff accommodation," I said. "Herbert Lightfoot told me there was a passage. Could we see it?"

"Of course, we will go via the ballroom," Angus said. "And thank you for the time you're spending on this investigation. I do appreciate it."

"We simply need to get to the bottom of this," I said.

We entered the ballroom and a member of staff was humming as she swept the floors. The tall windows were wide open with the heavy red velvet curtains pulled back, and the light streamed in making it look different to how it appeared in the evenings.

"Where did it happen?" Rose asked Angus.

He gestured ahead of us. "Just there, about three feet from the window."

I wondered whether it was possible for someone to hide behind the curtain, waiting to pounce.

Rose stepped forward, lowered her head, and spoke a soft prayer for her late husband. Angus glanced at me and we both also lowered our heads.

Once Rose had completed her words, Angus led us through an exit beside the small platform upon which the band usually played, then down a flight of stone steps to the lower floor. We passed two dressing rooms along the dark passage and then stopped at a closed door. Angus pulled the key from his pocket and unlocked it.

We went inside. It was rather untidy.

"Apologies." He gestured around the room. "I did not think to ask the maid to tidy before we came here." There was a sandwich with mould on it sitting upon a china plate on the desk. "I'd assumed the police would request access, but they didn't. I'm not sure if they even realised that he resided here at the hotel." He glanced at Rose who was looking around the room wide-eyed and blinking. "If there's anything you wish to take with you, I will ensure it's packaged and will cover the cost of transportation to London."

I glanced around the room. It was small, with a bed, desk, and a slim pine wardrobe unlike the rich mahogany of the large wardrobes in the suite I was staying in. Rose stared at the unmade bed and moved to the desk. As I looked down at the bed, I saw there was hair on the pillow. Whilst Micky had dark hair, it was certainly not as long as the hair I saw. Rose's attention was diverted as she opened a drawer in the desk, so I plucked the hair from the pillow, pulled the notebook from my bag and placed it within the sheets of the pages. I closed the book and then looked up. Angus watched me but made no comment.

"Do you think this is precious?" Rose asked as she turned around. In her hands was a handkerchief, upon which was a beautiful bracelet with emeralds set in gold. "It would be nice to imagine he'd bought this for me."

I gave her a sympathetic smile.

"No wonder he's not sent me any money recently." She lifted the bracelet. "He was clearly involved with someone and bought her this!"

Thinking of the hair I'd recovered from his pillow, I was inclined to agree but did not mention it. Rose's skin flushed and I did not want to upset her even more.

As she turned the bracelet in her hands, I spotted a brochure on the desk for the RMS Olympic, a ship which was one of a few in the White Star Line. Specifically, the brochure was on sailings of the transatlantic voyage to New York.

Angus picked it up. "That's the route Pearl took."

"Who's Pearl?" Rose asked.

"The female dancer, she left last week," I said.

"I never saw anything to suggest he and Pearl had a romantic connection," Angus said. "To be honest, Pearl never showed romantic interest in any man."

Rose gestured at the brochure. "Michel always dreamed of appearing on Broadway. I wouldn't have been surprised to find out he'd gone there."

"Transatlantic tickets are rather expensive," I said,

"By the looks of it," Rose said, "he's got a lover with expensive tastes." She sighed. "I think the Micky I knew died a long time ago, not last week. When he returned last, I felt I didn't know him any more. It was like having a stranger in the house."

She wrapped the bracelet up in the handkerchief. "I'll be selling it to pay for the kids' food and clothes. I certainly won't be wearing it."

"I can have it valued for you if you like?" I said, having visited a jeweller before in Bristol.

"That's kind of you," she said. "But I've a friend who works in Hatton Garden."

"Would you like me to place it in our safe for you?" Angus asked.

"Yes, please," she said with a smile as she handed it to Angus.

As Rose looked through Micky's belongings, locating items she felt her children may want, she stopped when she found a new passport.

She stared at the photograph on the document with a distant look then frowned. "The date of issue was the last time he came and visited us. I thought he actually wanted to see his kids. Looks like he just needed to get this from Clive House so he could make his escape!"

I knew the passport office was just across the Thames from where the White family lived. *Poor woman*, I thought.

"Maybe he was going stick to his legal name of Michael White in America. Probably yet another new personality, no doubt parading himself as an English gentleman," she scoffed then placed the document and birth certificate in her handbag. "I'm guessing the police will want to see these."

Once Rose had identified the possessions she intended to keep, Angus collected the small pile and said he would package them up for her. It was small enough for her to carry on the train home. He locked the door behind us and we made our way in silence back to the reception via another set of stairs, and Angus took the bracelet to store in the hotel safe.

"I guess I'd better get it over and done with," Rose

said. "And visit the police." She visibly shuddered. "I hope I don't have to identify him."

When we arrived at Branden Bay Police Station, my heart dropped as I spotted Inspector Stone alighting from a police car and walking up the steps before us. I was worried of what might become of Rose once he was aware of her presence.

I walked in to find him talking to Sergeant Chambers.

"Have there been any developments on the strangling?" Stone asked.

"You told us not to follow it up," Chambers said. "That the detained suspect was guilty."

"Ah, yes. But has any information come in at all? From that dratted woman."

"Inspector Stone," I said.

He swung around and his eyes shot open, and for a moment, he seemed unable to speak. I smiled to myself realising I had caught him off guard. His dark eyebrows knitted together in the pose I'd become accustomed to. "What do you want?"

"I'm bringing you information," I said with a small tight smile.

His eye twitched. I assumed he realised I had certainly overheard his comment to Sergeant Chambers.

"May I introduce you to Michel Blanc's wife, Mrs Rose White. In fact, the victim's name was not Michel

Blanc, after all, his legal name was Michael White. If you had bothered to search his room, you would have found his birth certificate and passport." I nodded at Rose who opened her bag and reached into it to retrieve the documents.

"He was from Lambeth," Rose said, handing the passport to Stone.

Stone stared at the passport then handed it to Chambers. "Take a statement." Then he turned and walked away.

Chambers gave a sympathetic smile to Rose. "Would you like a cup of tea? Then I'll take you through to an interview room."

"Do you need me to stay?" I asked her.

She shook her head. "I'll be fine."

Chambers addressed me. "The vicar's here with Mrs Flint." He gave me a grim look. "She's not in a good way."

"I wanted to visit her, is it not a good time?" I asked.

"I think she'll be pleased to see you. I'll get Ryan to take you in. Now come with me Mrs White, and I'll make you that cup of tea."

Ryan showed me to the cell, and as I entered Mrs Flint had a weak smile upon her face, but it was apparent from her red eyes that she'd been crying."

"Thank you so much for coming in," she said to me.

The vicar spoke to her in a hushed tone that I could not overhear before standing.

"Pleased to meet you," I said to him. "I'm Mrs Flint's

friend, Lady Ellen." I stretched out my hand and the vicar took it.

"Ah, yes, you're the wonderful woman I've been hearing so much about." He smiled. "Hopefully you'll bring this dreadful business to a close."

"I'll do my best," I said.

Once PC Ryan had escorted the vicar out, I sat beside Mrs Flint.

"Do you have any good news?" she asked with an expectant look on her face.

"We're making progress. We've discovered that Michel Blanc's real name was in fact Michael White, known as Micky, and we've located his wife. She's here, making a statement to Chambers, and it's the woman you saw with Micky the night he died."

"The lady called Rose?" she asked.

"Yes."

"Did she do it?" she asked, her eyes wide open.

"She said she was in Jake's Jazz Bar when the strangling occurred, although I've been unable to confirm her alibi, so cannot prove her innocence. She said she went there with a woman in her late thirties. She said the lady had dark hair. That was it. And there's been an interesting development which I need to follow up straight away."

"Yes?"

"Violet Sheringham was in the ballroom when Rose arrived. And Violet told me she was at home all evening, and so did her husband. I've also received information to suggested that Richard Sheringham wasn't at home at all, so Violet's alibi was a lie."

"Why did she lie to you?"

"That's exactly what I shall be asking her today, assuming she will speak to me."

Mrs Flint looked down at her hands. "Douglas hasn't been in yet. I just hope he's not spending all my money. If I knew I'd be coming in here, I would have opened my own account instead of adding my name to his."

Oh dear, I thought. Although I would not imagine Mr Flint being able to spend an entire two thousand pounds at The Branden Arms, I realised he might be spending a small portion of it. I found no point in worrying Mrs Flint any further, but realised the sooner I helped with her release from the cells, the better.

During our following conversation, Mrs Flint informed me that Norma Lloyd and John Breckon had visited her and were keeping her fed. Once we'd finished our conversation, I bade her farewell and assured her I was doing everything I could to aid her release. I knocked on the cell door and Ryan collected me.

"Stone's upstairs out of the way," he said as he led me up the corridor. "He's taking a bit more interest now, since you brought the wife in. He's with her now."

"I'm surprised he's here, considering the Vigilante Slasher claimed another victim."

"It's the Slasher attack that got him interested in this case. He's asked me to compile a list of any other unsolved strangling cases that have occurred in the past year, to look for a link."

"The inspector needs to simply interview those who were in Branden Bay at the time. Not every murderer has multiple victims like the Slasher," I said. "I understand the police failed to even search Micky White's room!"

"I wish he'd leave us to it, my lady," PC Ryan said. "Chambers says we'd do better without Scotland Yard's interference."

"I don't doubt that you're an extremely capable team when allowed to do your job."

I felt determined as I walked down the High Street and as soon as the pier came into view, I decided to go straight there. I wanted answers from Violet Sheringham.

CHAPTER 17

I pulled my coat to me as I walked along the wooden boards of the pier. The sun was hidden behind grey clouds, and I wondered whether we'd seen the last of summer. As I approached the entrance to the main pier building, I noticed that the shellfish stall, where Violet had complained about the smell of fish, was now closed.

As I entered the pier building, I found a few visitors inside, but Violet was not in view. I reached the office and knocked on the door.

Violet called out: "Come in!"

I opened the door. Violet stared at me, but did not immediately speak. She regarded me for a long moment, as if trying to read my mind from my expression. She previously had made no mention that she'd seen Micky the day he died, but as she had been spotted by Rose, I presumed that she must have expected at some point to be found out, even if she hoped she would not.

She gestured to the chair before her desk. "Please take a seat, my lady," she said after the period of silence.

"Thank you," I said, sensing that I was about to retrieve some important information from her. I had the impression that she wanted to talk, yet even as I sat down, she had not begun. I guessed she did not know where to start.

"You said you meet your husband at the theatre?" I asked.

She smiled. "I'd saved for months. My pay was low and to afford a nice dress and a decent seat took me a year. I wanted to pretend that for one night, I had something. To walk as others, do."

"I often find the inequalities in life uncomfortable," I said gently, wanting to let her know that I was not a woman of snobbery.

"You've never gone hungry. You've never feared what would become of you."

I'd feared uncertainty before, but it was not akin to what Violet referred to. I felt humbled.

She continued: "It was magical arriving at the theatre in a taxicab. I'd always loved the story Cinderella, and that's how I felt. I saw Richard in the foyer and he looked at me and held my gaze. It was as if he saw right inside me, he saw the real me, even though I looked nothing like the real me." She pulled a cigarette out of her case and lit it. "He was also there alone. It was his wedding anniversary, he used to go there with his first wife every year before she died." She smiled at me. "He told me it was love at first sight and fate." She took a drag of her cigarette perched on the end of the black holder. Her lips parted as the smoke wafted upwards into the air, hanging momentarily before it dispersed. It was as if she had practised it. Everything about this woman appeared to be about seduction and I realised I needed to be on my guard. I mustn't be taken in by anything which appeared untrue; after all she had already lied to me.

Violet gave a slow blink. "I didn't realise then, how my looks were perceived by men. Afterwards, in a bar, we talked for hours on all sorts of topics. I felt as if I was in another world." Her eyes glassed over. "And then he asked if he could walk me home. It was as if everything crashed down. How could I take him back to where I lived? I shared a bed with my sister and the house was so small. He'd already told me he owned the pier in Branden Bay and lived in a grand apartment overlooking the sea. I was in floods of tears before I could even think of an excuse." She looked at me. "He said he could tell I was of the working classes, and that did not bother him at all. Even though I'd been so careful with my speech." She laughed. "I've since had many elocution lessons."

"I find local accents charming," I said.

"They define us, Lady Ellen. You have no idea."

I felt that I did, as I'd been watching life through Lottie's eyes, but made no comment. "You were then married to Mr Sheringham?"

"Yes, in a short space of time. His mother was unhappy, but I worked hard and she soon accepted me. I work many hours here, at the pier. I know there's a large gap in our ages, but I love Richard." She paused as if unsure whether to continue.

"It must have been hard," I said.

"My family were poor and my father sick much of the time, so we all had to work, unlike your upbringing I'm sure," Violet said. "The hours were long, I was in the processing plant near the harbour. Fish was brought in from Wales and Cornwall. It was often cold and wet, although that was better than the hot days, when some were rotten." She took a deep breath. "It's as if I'll never rid myself of the smell."

I felt guilty at having previously judged her as petulant, realising she would have worked long hours in the cold, gutting, cleaning, and preparing from a young age. *No wonder she hates the smell of fish,* I thought. "What made you decide to change your life? I asked.

"I was attacked one day on the way home from work."

"That's awful," I said, feeling worse for being judgmental.

"I narrowly escaped falling into the harbour. Luckily, I was taught how to defend myself by my brothers. I threw off the assailant. I don't know where the strength came from, but it was like an inner rage overtook me and said, 'I'm not standing for this'. The man soon found himself in the water. As I watched him floundering and cursing me, I ran away. I heard his strokes as he swam to the edge and I ran so fast, imagining he would kill me if he caught me. I decided there and then that to survive life, I needed to change it."

"Why did your husband say he was with you at home on Sunday, when he was not?"

She blinked, clearly taken aback by my interruption. As rude as it was, I did not want to find myself deep in her spell.

"I've had it confirmed," I said, "that he was at The Branden Arms playing the roulette. Apparently, he is there for a private event every Sunday evening."

Violet stubbed her cigarette in the ashtray and regarded me. It was as if she'd expected me to find out. That she'd waited for this moment. I also expected that she had rehearsed her answer. "He wanted to protect me, isn't that obvious? Do you not have a man who would do anything for you?"

I did not answer and waited for her to continue but she did not. At that moment, I thought I should clarify why I was there. "You met Michel's wife the day he died."

Her lips slightly parted, but she remained silent.

"She described you perfectly as the woman who was at The Grand in the ballroom that evening. Her story differs to yours, as you told me you were at home with your husband, asleep. She has given your description to the police."

"She really was Michel's wife?" she asked in a near whisper.

"Yes, her name is Rose," I said. "Rose White. Michel

was in fact not French, but an actor and entertainer called Micky White from Lambeth, London."

"He pretended to be French?" The surprise on her face was natural, the gentle manner she'd used when playing the part of a woman victimised was lost.

"Yes," I said.

"He lied to me?" she said in a more forceful voice to the gentle one she had been using.

"It was true that he performed at the London Palladium," I said.

"Was he going to keep up the French façade all the way to America?"

"America?" I repeated.

She paused for a moment. "I was not joining him, if that's what you are imagining. But Michel had been begging me for weeks to leave Richard and accompany him to America. I, of course, refused. He said he had the money to pay for the ship, albeit a lower-class ticket, and that we would have a comfortable life as he had been accepted into a Broadway show. That I would love America." She picked another cigarette out of her silver case and affixed it to her holder. "He'd asked to see me the night he died. I arrived at the ballroom and he became nasty when I refused to go to America with him. He threatened to spread the details of my past and said that I was a common fish gutter. I lost my temper and shouted at him. I made it clear that I'd never leave Richard for him, and told him to leave me alone, otherwise he'd regret it."

"How did he react?" I asked.

"He apologised and became upset. Asked me to forgive him. He suddenly seemed so vulnerable and he looked into my eyes and kissed me on the forehead. I think he'd accepted in that moment that I was never going to leave Richard and it hurt him. And then the door opened, which took me by surprise as it was at least ten minutes until his next lesson was scheduled. It was the woman, who said she was his wife! I couldn't believe it."

"So you truly thought he was French?" I asked.

"He spoke in a French accent all of the time even when...um..." She faltered and in that moment, I guessed it was her hair I'd found on his pillow.

"He lied to a lot of people," I said gently. "Especially his wife. He had children."

She stopped fiddling with her cigarette and stared at me. "I don't believe it. What sort of man does that?"

"How did he know you used to gut fish?" I asked.

"I stayed up with him one evening talking." She ran a hand over her forehead and I guessed it was more than one evening. "He told me about his earlier life in France." She gave a short laugh. "All of it clearly fictitious. And I shared my history, the truth of it." She stopped. "I should not be telling you this. Maybe you should leave."

"I need to discover the truth," I said. "It appears from what you're telling me, that you had a close relationship with Micky."

Violet's face flushed red and her voice increased in volume. "I admit it, I'm relieved he's dead. Richard had been pressuring me to start a family. I thought all he wanted was a baby and that was why he wanted a young wife and didn't care if I was from a lowly background. He could dress me up, refine me. Pay for beauty treatments and creams to heal my hands." She showed me her palms. "Just so I could produce a child to inherit the pier. A child his first wife was unable to give him. I was angry at that and wanted to make him jealous. That's all."

We heard a creak outside.

Violet whispered to me, "Is someone there?"

"I'll check." I stood up and opened the door and saw Richard Sheringham marching away. *Oh dear,* I thought. I turned back into the room. "I'm afraid it was your husband."

"Now I have even more explaining to do," she said. "I may not be sad that Michel has gone, but I didn't kill him. Now, if you will excuse me, I must speak to my husband."

I thanked Violet for her honesty, hoping that she was indeed being honest. I now felt the need to speak to Eddie at The Grand.

CHAPTER 18

"*L*ady Ellen, what can I get you?" Eddie asked as I approached the bar at The Grand Hotel.

"A glass of Bordeaux please," I said.

He poured from an open bottle then passed me the glass. I took a sip of the deep red wine. It was at a perfect temperature and had a warmth that I always found comforting, for it reminded me of home – having been my father's favourite drink.

I glanced intently at Eddie. "Have you seen Rose White since she arrived at the hotel?"

His eyes darted from left to right. He was clearly wondering how to proceed.

"I'm aware that you know her," I said when he failed to reply. "What I don't understand is why you omitted to mention that to me when we spoke?"

"I didn't want trouble. She's had enough to put up with being married to Micky. At least she's got a life insurance pay out coming, that's the only good thing he ever did for her."

Life insurance? I thought and paused for a moment. Rose White had kept that to herself!

"If I was her," Eddie said, "I'd be out of here as soon as I got the death certificate."

I took another sip of my wine. "I understand you knew Rose was here, the day Micky died!"

He hesitated and did not comment.

"It appears there are a few facts you've kept from us. Such as the fact that he was English and from London."

Eddie moved to the other end of the bar to serve a customer. I watched him, then he returned to me.

"How did you find out?" he asked.

"From your ex-colleagues at the London Palladium, and you also confided in the Simpson sisters," I said.

"Ah yes," he chuckled. "I did get rather drunk with them one evening. They could drink Lightfoot under the table. When I got here, Micky recognised me and told me not to tell anyone his real name, or that he had a wife back in London."

"Were you blackmailing him?" I thought I would get straight to the point. "Is that why he pulled you by the scruff of your neck across the bar?"

"I wouldn't call it that, but he lashed out at me after asking me to return some money he'd loaned me. I said it would be a shame if people were to find out he was a fake."

"That sounds a lot like blackmail to me!" I said with

a shake of my head. "It also appears that you owe an amount to Mr Lightfoot."

"He said he wanted me to pay him back in drink."

I lowered my voice. "Alcohol from the hotel no doubt."

"Are you going to tell Mr Scott?" He looked around to see if he could see his employer. Before I could answer, he looked over my shoulder. "Ah, Miss Simpson."

"Hello Eddie, dear," Betty said then turned to me. "Are you having a lovely day?" She continued without waiting for my reply. "I've been sitting by the window of my room, having a tipple with Nelly, watching the tide coming in."

"Would you like a drink, Betty?" Eddie asked.

She nodded with tears in her eyes.

"Are you well?" I asked her as Eddie made her drink.

"The dancer's death has set me off. I've been remembering my poor Luke." She sighed. "You're a good boy, Eddie," she said as he returned and handed her a drink. "I'd have loved to have had a son like you. What will you do next with your life?"

"Ah, I don't know Miss Simpson. I want to see a bit more of the country before I settle."

I considered the young man needed to learn a measure of responsibility and hoped before he departed, he would settle his debts.

"Why don't you come along with Nelly and me when we move on. We've heard Torquay is beautiful with peaceful beaches and blue waters. The town has visitors all year. There are hotels and seaside bars. There's an artistic crowd too, people from your way, in London."

"It sounds great," Eddie said with a grin.

"I'm sure you'd easily find a job," Betty said. "Everyone loves you."

Eddie was called to serve another customer. I was not as convinced that he was as angelic as Betty painted him.

"Why don't we sit at that table by the window," I said and linked my arm in hers. Her bloodshot eyes were framed by her spectacles and her gaze told me that she had enjoyed more than one small tipple in her room.

Once I found a free table, we sat down and Betty gazed out of the window. "Oh to be young, if I had my time again." Tears brimmed in her eyes. "Things would have been different with Luke. I miss him."

I felt terrible at the sorrow she displayed. I handed her a clean handkerchief from my bag. "Here, take this. I'm so sorry you lost him."

She took the handkerchief and wiped her eyes. "I'll never forgive myself."

"What for?" I asked.

She looked up at me, her eyes wide, and she seemed so much younger, as if I was looking at her younger self. "He died thinking I had no love for him at all. And that's not the case...I..." She stopped and took a deep breath and wiped her nose. "I'm sorry. Don't pay attention to me, the drink is talking. But if you want a happy life, my lady, make sure you tell those you love the contents of your heart."

I looked to my right to find Hamilton approaching, and the letter in my bag again came to my attention. What if something were to happen to Hamilton during high seas? What if he died not knowing how I felt?

"Ellen, good news," he said as he reached my table.

"Good news is always welcome," I said, and then behind him I saw Mrs Flint being helped into the hotel bar by Mrs Lloyd.

"There she is," Norma said, gesturing in my direction. "Now take a seat and I'll get you a brandy."

"Allow me to fetch the drink, Mrs Lloyd," Hamilton said, pulling out a chair at my table for Mrs Flint to be seated and then another for Norma.

"I'm so pleased they released you," I said. "Did the Inspector finally come to his senses?"

"Someone confessed to the murder. That's what PC Ryan said. He brought us down here in the car. I wanted to see you immediately to say that you can stop your enquiries. I've wasted enough of your time." She beamed at me. "And I'm so grateful."

"It's no trouble," I said. "Who confessed?"

"I've been told not to say." She glanced at Betty and across to Hamilton at the bar.

"It was Richard Sheringham," Norma said with a sniff.

"I told you not to repeat it," Mrs Flint said to Norma.

She ignored the comment. "He told the police that he'd done it during a jealous rage."

"Well, I never," Betty said.

"Sorry for my rudeness," I said. "May I introduce Miss Betty Simpson, she's a resident at the hotel. And these are my good friends Mrs Ina Flint and Mrs Norma Lloyd."

Betty leaned forward. "I saw them arrest you here, dear. I'm so pleased this ordeal is over for you."

"John's gone to fetch the motorcar from Millar's then we're taking Ina back there," Norma said.

"You're not going home to your house?" I asked Mrs Flint.

She lowered her head.

"I told Ina, she needs looking after properly until she gets her strength back," Norma said. "John went around to tell Douglas that they were preparing to let her go and the place is a stinking pit." Norma shook her head.

"He's upset," Mrs Flint said. "It's been hard for him, thinking I killed a man. I went behind his back, he's entitled to worry that I was romancing someone else. It's not his fault if he's in a bad way."

I made no comment as my sympathy for Douglas Flint had run out.

"Once you've cleaned up and have a decent meal inside you, we'll have a talk about that husband of yours," Norma said. I gathered from the tone of her voice that she very much thought Mr Flint was letting his wife down.

Betty smiled as her sister approached. "Nelly, someone's confessed to Micky White's murder." After we had made our introductions, Nelly pulled another chair over and sat beside her sister.

Hamilton passed Mrs Flint her brandy.

"Thank you," she said and drank most of it in one gulp. "I don't know what to do. I don't know if me and Douglas can have a marriage after what I've done."

"Ina Flint, don't speak like that," Norma said. "He's never been a great husband. What about when he was carrying on with Mabel and said he was leaving you for her!"

"That was years ago, when Joe was tiny," Mrs Flint snapped. "It wasn't his fault. A man has his needs and he said he doesn't ever want to talk about that again. He feels ashamed, and I'm surprised you brought that up at a time like this."

Norma softened her voice. "All I'm saying is, he's no saint."

"Thank you, Lady Ellen, for what you did for me," Mrs Flint said, her face flushed, clearly unhappy that her marriage was a topic for discussion. She finished the last of the brandy.

"I'm so pleased you've been freed," I said, although I was wondering who this woman called Mabel was! In addition to this, I felt a growing concern that Richard Sheringham was not really the killer. Was he simply protecting his wife?

Breckon arrived and Mrs Flint rose to standing.

"Oh," Norma said to me. "We didn't get those jobs in Minehead."

"Something better will come along," I said as Breckon reached us. "Or you might find things settle a little at Millar's."

Breckon gave a grim nod. "We wouldn't have felt happy leaving Mrs Flint in her time of need. So, it's for the best."

"It's good to feel needed," Norma added. "We've felt like spare parts up at Millar's."

I watched them leave, so pleased that Mrs Flint was finally free and that I could return to Ashcombe without that worry.

"Who'd have thought Mr Sheringham would do such a thing," Nelly said.

"Jealousy can drive some men crazy," Hamilton said.

"It's a shame, as he appears to be such a caring husband," Betty said.

"Micky White had a lot to answer for," Nelly said. "I almost feel sorry for Mr Sheringham."

I was sceptical of Mr Sheringham's confession and even though Mrs Flint was free, I still felt I wanted to talk through what had happened to the dancer. I had a few more days in Branden Bay and felt I owed it to Angus to tie up the loose ends.

I asked Hamilton to accompany me and we left the sisters chatting to Mrs Flint whilst she and Norma waited for Breckon to pick them up.

As we reached the reception, Lottie and Sebastian were arriving back having taken Prince for a run. My dog wagged his tail as soon as he saw me and I felt a pang of guilt at having neglected him. I informed them of Ina Flint's release and that I wished to discuss it in my suite.

ONCE WE WERE SEATED and Lottie had the notebook in her hand, which I'd briefly read through, we began our discussions.

"Richard Sheringham has confessed to the murder of Michel Blanc, real name Micky White," I said. "But I don't think it's him, considering he is the only suspect who has a verifiable alibi."

"Agreed," Hamilton said. "At the time of the murder, he was in The Branden Arms playing roulette."

"So why did he confess?" Lottie asked.

To protect his wife," I said.

"Which would make Violet Sheringham a strong possibility," Hamilton added.

"I reckon she was having an affair with Micky White!" Lottie said as she wrote Violet's name on the page. "After the way they carried on that evening on the dance floor."

"It wasn't decent the way they danced in front of Mr Sheringham like that," Sebastian added. "The poor chap."

"Maybe Violet wanted her husband to kill Micky," I said. "And when he didn't, she decided to do it herself. When I spoke to Violet earlier today, she told me that she was not upset that Micky was dead and I believed her. Richard Sheringham was listening to our conversation. I'm not sure exactly how much he overheard, but he may have well deduced from what was said, that his wife is guilty."

"He might know she's guilty," Hamilton said. "And realised you were close to the truth. What else did Mrs Sheringham say?"

"I asked her why she lied to me about her alibi when she was placed in the ballroom that evening," I said. "Violet said it was true that they were in close proximity, but she said she merely felt sorry for Micky who had asked her to leave her husband and she'd refused."

"Once someone tells one lie, they tell a whole string of them," Hamilton muttered with a shake of his head.

"I discussed her past; she had a tough childhood working from an early age in a fish processing plant. She met Richard Sheringham at the theatre having saved for a ticket and suitable attire and in her words – he rescued her." I paused and glanced at Hamilton. "She said it was love at first sight."

"It seems extremely plausible that Sheringham would lie to protect his wife," Hamilton said.

"Is Rose still a suspect?" Lottie asked.

"Absolutely not," Hamilton said. "She's a good, God-fearing woman."

"I'm afraid she had a motive," I said. "Eddie let slip that there's an insurance policy which Rose will benefit from as soon as she collects the death certificate."

"She didn't mention an insurance policy in London!" Sebastian said.

"Do we know that Eddie is speaking the truth?" Hamilton asked. "I'm a little wary of him as he appears to have much to say about others. As if he's constantly deflecting the attention from himself."

"From my discussions with him, he admitted to blackmailing Micky," I said. "Although he did not call it that name, he told Micky that he would expose his true identity if he insisted on chasing him for repayment of the money he had loaned him."

"How much did he owe the chap?" Sebastian asked.

"I've no idea," I said. "However, Micky was planning to leave for America so may have been desperate for the money. It's possible that there was a confrontation that night in the ballroom, that Eddie entered and left unseen via the staff entrance, and that it was him that used Mrs Flint's forgotten scarf to strangle the man."

"What was his alibi again?" Lottie asked as she updated the page.

"He hasn't got one," Hamilton said. "He said he was alone in his room."

"What about Herbert Lightfoot?" Lottie asked.

"He's benefited greatly from Micky's demise," Hamilton said. "I'd say the chap has had a new lease of life."

"What was Lightfoot's alibi?" Sebastian asked.

"He said he was in The Branden Arms all evening," I said. "We need to clarify that with Mrs Kerr."

"Who do you consider to be the guilty party, Ellen?" Sebastian asked.

"I'm afraid that Mrs Sheringham is top of my list," I

said, "If her husband is prepared to lose his life over this murder, we cannot ignore the fact that he feels she's capable of strangling a man."

Hamilton shook his head. "I find it difficult to comprehend."

"When I spoke to her, she informed me that she'd been taught how to protect herself by her brothers," I said. "And recalled how she'd defended herself against an attacker who ended up in Bristol harbour after she had fought him off."

"We've still got a lot of suspects," Lottie said writing in the notebook.

"It must be one of them," Sebastian said. "We simply need to keep our noses to the ground."

I sighed. "It's a big hotel with many guests. The killer may not even be on our suspect list. There have been many references to a dark-haired woman – it could be someone else staying at the hotel." I felt extremely sorry for Angus having an unsolved strangling at The Grand, especially when his wife was due back so soon.

Lottie looked up from the notebook. "What's our next move?"

"As urgent as the matter is, I feel we could all do with a rest from this." I smiled at Hamilton. "I'm hankering after a country drive."

CHAPTER 19

*T*he following morning, I felt somewhat freer having decided to have a day away from Branden Bay. Lottie and I had breakfast in the suite. Sebastian had taken Prince out for his walk to tire him as I'd decided to drive us in my motorcar. Hamilton had arranged for it to be washed and the oil and petrol checked. I was rather excited about the drive, as in Branden Bay I had no use for it as everything was within walking distance. There was a knock at the door. Lottie opened it and Prince charged in, looking less than worn out – indeed, he looked even more excited than he did before his run along the beach. Sebastian, however, was frowning.

"Is there something the matter?" I asked.

"There've been complaints that guests have had items stolen from their rooms," he said.

"There's a thief in the hotel?" Lottie asked.

"A few guests have reported items missing over the

past couple of weeks, but today it's the Simpson sisters and three other rooms." He paused. "I spoke with Mr Scott and he said that the police suspect an inside job and will be questioning the staff."

"I'm glad that we'll be away today," I said, and I was also pleased that I had kept my valuables in the hotel safe. "How are the sisters?"

"When I left them they were on their way up to their room, but they took the lift. They're on this floor I believe?"

"Yes," I said. "Close to the lift."

"We'll have to see them before we leave, Ellen," Lottie said.

"I know, but do not get caught up in it, Lottie. We all need a calm day together." I was desperate for a day spent with Hamilton. An entire day during which we could relax. I checked my wristwatch. "Ernest said he would bring the car around to the front of the hotel for us at half past, so we have twenty minutes."

Sebastian agreed to meet us at the car. When we reached the Simpson sisters' room, the door was ajar and Lottie tapped gently. Nelly had her arm around Betty's shoulders as they sat on one of the twin beds.

"We thought we would pop in to check on you," I said. "We heard you've been burgled."

"The wedding ring," Betty said. "It means the world to me. It's a symbol of love." She descended into sobs.

"Our mother's ring," Nelly added, her face grim. "Betty is the custodian of it and wears it on a chain around her neck, but removed it before she bathed yesterday and left it on the dressing table. We didn't notice it was missing last night, but it was gone this morning."

"Hopefully the police will find it for you," Lottie said.

"Don't give up hope," I added, although deep down I doubted that something so small would be recovered.

"I can't believe they did it in broad daylight," Betty said through tears. "Three rooms robbed on this floor and one on the floor below."

"I guess they never came in our room because of Prince," Lottie said.

I walked over to the dressing table to view where she had left her ring and spotted something laying on the shiny surface – a long brown hair. *Not another brunette?* I thought as I picked it up. Certainly, the wrong shade to belong to Nelly or Betty. *I shall mention that to the police and Angus,* I thought. It would appear they were looking for a woman with dark hair, but I kept it to myself. I did not want the Simpson sisters accusing every brunette they saw in the hotel.

I turned around as Betty continued to sob.

"You need to brighten up," Nelly said. "We're leaving in half an hour to catch the boat to Bristol with Walter."

Betty sat up and brightened her face. It appeared that the mention of Major Fitzwilliam had at least ceased her tears.

"Hopefully it will turn up," she said with a watery smile."

. . .

WE HURRIED down the stairs after collecting Prince, as we were now running late and I knew Hamilton and Sebastian would be waiting for us. As we reached the reception, I saw Angus Scott looking extremely flustered.

He approached us. "Lady Ellen, what must you think of your stay here? I can confirm we're putting a guard on every floor and searching the staff rooms until the perpetrator has been found."

"I think, Angus, that you will be looking for a woman with dark hair. I found this long brown hair in the Simpson sisters' room." I passed it over, contained in a sheet of writing paper. "Unless the usual maid has hair that colour?"

He opened the paper and studied the hair. "No, the maid for the third floor has fair hair. It must belong to the thief." He gave me a wry smile. "You are most observant, my lady. I hope that you have an enjoyable day, Captain Hamilton advised me you are visiting Penderley House?"

"Yes we are, and we must leave as the captain is waiting for us outside." I turned and spotted Rose walking through the reception.

"Lady Ellen," she said. "Have you had something stolen?"

"No, Prince is a good guard dog." I patted his head.

My dog barked hearing his name.

She smiled at him. "What a lovely dog."

"And how are you?" I asked politely, mindful that I didn't have time to chat.

"I've been arranging the funeral. I'll bury Micky here and then hold a memorial service back at St Mary-at-Lambeth." She gestured towards the exit. "I'm off to the staff exit now to meet one of the assistant cooks, she's already been interviewed and it's her day off. I've eaten breakfast in the staff dining room. They're all so nice, it's a shame one of them might be a thief."

"Hopefully the police will get to the bottom of it soon," I said.

I watched Rose leave and wondered whether I should have quizzed her on the life insurance policy, to check whether Eddie was being truthful about that. However, I'd promised myself a case-free day. *It will have to wait,* I thought.

As we stepped outside, Hamilton and Sebastian were standing beside my motorcar. I smiled as I took in the blue paint which made it stand out from many other vehicles.

"Do you wish me to drive?" Hamilton asked me.

"No thank you, I'm looking forward to doing so myself," I said, then noticed there was a huge picnic basket tied to the back of the car. I smiled at Hamilton.

"I asked Chef Moreau to prepare us a luncheon. It's a thank you, for everything you've done for me and others in a selfless fashion." He glanced upwards. "The weather appears fair."

"Thank you so much, Ernest." I approached my blue

Rolls-Royce which gleamed. The chrome had been polished so much it appeared like mirrors. The roof was pulled up against the fresh sea air, which was sensible with the September weather often changeable. Sebastian and Lottie climbed inside first, taking the back seat with Prince between them. Ernest opened the driver's door for me and I took my seat. He was soon in the passenger seat, adjusting his cap and gloves. I adored driving, especially on mornings like that, and as I started the engine, I felt the stresses of the recent days lift.

I ran my hand over the leather of the steering wheel. I loved to feel the wheel in my hands and only wore driving gloves on the chilliest of days.

"Are we all ready?" I called over my shoulder, glancing in the rear-view mirror. Lottie nodded, whilst Sebastian gazed at her and Prince gave an excited bark. I smiled; he was always so eager for an adventure and I was pleased that he would be able to run on the fields of the Penderly estate. With everyone settled, I started the car and the engine came to life. We were soon heading along Beach Road towards the Bristol Road which lead us out of Branden Bay. It was the perfect morning for a drive to Penderly House.

The journey took less time than I'd imagined. We wound our way along hedge-lined lanes. As we neared Penderly, I spotted the chimneys before we could see the house itself, rising above the trees as if they were peeking over the top at us. When I reached the gravel drive, the sound of the crunching beneath the wheels reminded me of home. Penderly's ivy-covered façade helped the building blend into the surrounding woodland and fields. My own home had no such greenery and was more of a grand building, whereas Penderly had a peaceful atmosphere. I pulled the car to a stop close to the entrance, where a lawn spread out, edged by neatly trimmed bushes.

"Travelling always makes me hungry," Sebastian said as we exited the car.

"I understand there are benches within the trees, where we can eat," Hamilton said.

"I'll take the basket," Sebastian said as Hamilton removed the straps that had held it in place.

After a short walk, we found a row of benches, two of which were already occupied. After selecting one, Hamilton opened the basket and we removed the plates, cutlery and food. There was also a bottle of champagne and glasses.

"This is so beautiful," I said as Sebastian and Lottie chattered over the fillings of the sandwiches. There were also cold meats, salad and an array of cakes and biscuits. Hamilton opened the champagne with a pop and we all toasted Penderly.

Prince ate the Spratt's dog food we'd brought for him, then sat with his nose twitching as he stared at a slice of roast chicken. I allowed him a piece and as he chewed it, his tail thumped on the ground.

After we'd eaten, we took a leisurely stroll around the grounds and then towards the house and we were met by a guide.

"Good afternoon," he said to us as we approached. "Would you like to know the history of the house?"

"We certainly would," Sebastian said.

"The main house dates back to the seventeenth century," he said. "It was built by the Penderly family. The last heir, Lord Frederick Penderly, had no children to pass it on to and the house had fallen into decline. Lord Penderly knew his wider family would be unable to afford the renovations and he did not want it to be sold on and possibly demolished, so he bequeathed it to the National Trust. He wished the estate to continue to be a place of beauty and history, open for others to appreciate."

I felt a lump form in my throat. The reason I'd visited Penderly was that I had been considering donating Ashcombe Hall to the National Trust. As much as I loved my home, it had felt a burden weighing down on me. My staff were not getting any younger and I had asked myself during my time away whether I wanted to spend the rest of my days tied to Ashcombe. I had more than enough investments for a comfortable life and the hall was self-sufficient and could possibly be managed by the trust. And the hall could be preserved so that visitors could see how my family had lived over the generations. Even if one day I had children, I would not necessarily wish to burden them with the responsibility that I felt restricted my life.

"Are you well, Ellen?" Hamilton asked me.

I blinked, realising I had been deep in thought. "Yes, I'm simply struck by the beauty of the place." I did not want to share my thoughts for fear of expressing too much emotion. Maybe spending time with Hamilton and Lottie had urged me to hanker after a simpler life.

"Shall we go inside?" Sebastian asked eagerly with Lottie holding his hand.

Hamilton offered me his arm and we followed them inside.

CHAPTER 20

The following day I felt so completely rested. We'd all been extremely tired when we'd returned from Penderly, so we'd shared high tea in my suite before the men retired to their room and we all took an early night. After we'd eaten breakfast, we decided to collect Prince for a morning stroll when Betty approached us in the reception. She had a broad smile upon her face.

"Lady Ellen, Sergeant Chambers thinks they have my ring up at the police station." She beamed at me.

"Would you like me to accompany you?" I asked. After the break away from the mystery, I felt a renewed energy to solve the murder and was keen to discover whether the police truly believed Richard Sheringham was guilty.

"Oh yes please, dear. I need to collect my bag."

I turned to my companions. "Do you mind awfully if I accompany Betty to the police station?"

"That's perfectly fine," Hamilton said. "I do hope they recover your ring." He smiled at Betty and I wondered whether he was warming to her or whether he was simply feeling much more relaxed after our jaunt to Penderly House. I certainly was.

Having taken the lift up to the third floor with Betty, she opened her bedroom door. "Nelly's not feeling too well," she said, pointing to Nelly asleep in the chair facing the lit fire.

"Has she a chill?" I asked.

"Maybe," she whispered. "Let's leave her. She's also got one of her headaches and she's not stopped criticising me for losing Mother's ring. She said I should not have removed it from my neck. It would be a great surprise if I came back with it."

Nelly let out a loud snore.

Betty gave a giggle. "I'll fetch my handbag."

We then popped along to my suite and I collected my own bag.

As we waited for the lift, Betty smiled at me. "Do you think the Major will want to come with us?"

Ah, I understand, I thought, realising exactly why she didn't want to wake her sister. Betty clearly had romance on her mind. It had been heart-warming to see the friendship grow between her and the Major. "Shall we check his room?" I asked.

"It's on the second floor. Room twelve."

After knocking on the Major's bedroom door, there was no reply.

Betty sighed. "Maybe he went for a stroll?" Her

disappointment was evident. "Let's go and see if they have Mother's ring. I do hope it's there. I've felt awful ever since it went missing."

It was a slow walk and I had wondered whether I should have offered to drive. I did not rush, as Betty always walked at a sedate pace. She looked into one of the shop windows as we headed up the High Street.

"Is there something we can buy Lottie before you leave?" she asked me. "I've taken to her. I've often wondered what it would be like to have a daughter." Her voice broke. I felt as if I was staring at my older self, filled with regrets. Alone, with no family.

I pushed the thought from my mind. "Lottie will be spending much time writing to Sebastian over the coming months, so attractive writing paper would be ideal." Betty went inside and selected writing paper with a floral pattern upon it. I realised that I too needed a great deal of paper to write to Hamilton, although back at the hall I had my own embossed writing paper. It would appear much too formal for a personal letter to the man I held affection for, so I also purchased some paper and as I deposited it into my bag.

We finally reached the police station and approached the desk.

"Lady Ellen, did you have something stolen?" Chambers asked with a frown, his face was flushed.

"Is everything well?" I enquired.

He hesitated. "It's the job, my lady. It's sometimes difficult."

I didn't press him further. "Thankfully I have no missing items, however, I'm here to support Miss Simpson."

Chambers smiled at Betty. "I think you're in luck!"

He led us into an interview room where there were tables laid out with items upon them, with someone already inspecting them. Chambers went in before us.

"Chambers." Inspector Stone's voice boomed from outside the room.

"I'll leave you with Jones," Chambers said to me, gesturing at the police officer.

It was then that I noticed that the woman PC Jones was assisting was Violet Sheringham.

Betty looked to me and raised her eyebrows.

"You were right, it's not here," Violet said, then reached for her handkerchief. "My husband's in the cells and my bracelet is lost." She then noticed us, gave me a stony glare and left with her head down.

I watched her go, wondering whether she blamed me for her husband's arrest. "Has Mrs Sheringham lost something?" I asked PC Jones.

"A bracelet," he said as Betty went to the table to look for her ring. "An emerald bracelet, with diamonds too. The thief may have already sold that on. She said she lost it the other week at The Grand and as the perpetrator is a member of staff, believed it might have been with the items recovered."

I thought back to the emerald bracelet we'd found in Micky's room, and since placed in The Grand

Hotel's safe. It appeared to be a bit of a coincidence. *Did Micky steal it from her?* I wondered.

"And how is Mr Sheringham?" I asked, but before he replied Betty interrupted.

"There it is," she said with tears in her eyes as she picked up the ring hanging on a gold chain.

"Would you like me to put it on you?" I asked.

"No need," she said as she swiftly put it around her neck, fastened it and then lifted it to her lips and kissed it. "Thank you so much, PC Jones."

"I'm glad we recovered it for you. Everyone's been asked to look at all of the items," he said, "in case something was stolen that they're not yet aware of. You should both check, because if there's anything left, we'll be asking the rest of the guests at the hotel to take a look."

Betty walked along the line and I followed. She hesitated and looked at each in turn, as did I. There were a few designer hats, a lot of jewellery items and various ID documents. This was a thief who knew what they could sell on.

I looked over to PC Jones. "I wouldn't be surprised if the thief had a history, they seem to be well aware of resaleable items."

He lowered his voice. "We suspect a crime ring."

"It's sad when people get drawn in," I said.

"Who was it?" Betty asked.

"I'm not at liberty to say," he said, standing to attention.

I looked at the passports and picked one of them up.

Taverham, I thought as I read the name. *I've heard that somewhere before.* I opened the passport as the door opened and glanced at the stern looking picture of Mrs Juliet Taverham. *Another brunette,* I thought.

"Jones," Chambers bellowed from the corridor, sounding rather stressed. He was usually a calm man.

"If you'll excuse me," PC Jones said.

"Can you lock this room please," Chambers said from the doorway. "We need you to cover the front desk."

We followed Jones out of the room and as we reached the front desk, it was to the sounds of a voice I recognised. I stopped in my tracks as PC Ryan was cuffing a shocked looking Mrs Flint whilst Norma stood by sobbing.

"What on earth is going on here?" I asked.

"Mrs Flint is being taken to Horfield Prison," Inspector Stone said. "And she will need to seek profession legal help. Not an amateur."

"You already released her," I said. "This is preposterous." I was disturbed by the defeatist expression on Mrs Flint's face.

"She's being charged with another strangulation. Of Mr Douglas Flint."

"It wasn't me!" Mrs Flint said as if in physical pain. "Why would I do that?"

"He's dead?" I gasped. I looked to Betty whose eyes were wide open as she adjusted her glasses.

"No, he's alive and at the hospital," Norma said, wiping her eyes.

"How is he?" I asked, somewhat relieved that the man had not been murdered.

"He'll live," Norma said as if she was not at all concerned about her friend's husband. Clearly Norma was no fan of Douglas Flint. "And she never done it, I keep telling you." She gestured at Inspector Stone. "She's been with me all morning."

"So you say," Stone growled. "Her house is only yards from the hotel, and she was identified."

We went outside, Norma still sobbed and Mrs Flint wailed in a high pitch as they bundled her into a police van with bars at the windows.

Betty placed a comforting hand on my back. I was so grateful that she was there.

I watched the van rumble away, as Mrs Flint stared out the back window. "I can't believe I've let her down," I said as my chin trembled.

Betty put her arm around me. "It's not your fault, dear."

"You're a loving and caring woman, Ellen," Norma said through a sob. "Don't blame yourself."

I felt stunned, as if a member of my own family had been taken away.

John Breckon drove us back to The Grand Hotel using Millar's motorcar. We travelled in silence, and when we arrived it was to find Major Fitzwilliam in the cards room, looking somewhat dishevelled. Betty looked at him and hesitated.

"Go, on," I said. "I'm sure Nelly can wait a little

while longer. She did appear awfully tired." I wanted to slip back to the suite to catch my breath.

"Will you be okay?" Norma asked. "We need to get back to work else we'll be getting laid off earlier than I imagined."

"Yes of course, and Norma, I can assure you I will do everything I can for Ina."

ONCE INSIDE MY SUITE, Prince bounded over for a stroke.

Lottie's jaw dropped when she saw me. "Ellen, what's wrong? Did Betty not find her ring?"

"Yes, she did. But Mr Flint is in hospital following an attempt on his life and Ina has been rearrested and taken to prison."

"Oh, my goodness," Lottie said. "I wonder if Joe knows what's going on. Maybe we should write to him?"

"He will be devastated to find his father in hospital and his mother in Horfield." I sighed.

There was a rap on the door and Lottie opened it to find Sebastian and Hamilton.

"PC Ryan has been here," Sebastian said. "About the burglaries, but before he left he took us to one side and told us the bad news about about Mr Flint!"

"I'm already aware that there was an attempt on his life and Ina has been taken to prison, but do you have any more details?" I asked.

Hamilton nodded. "Mr Flint was asleep in his chair and woke to find a scarf around his neck. He said he was pretty sure the strangler was his wife. The postman visited and looked through the window as he came up the garden path and interrupted the strangler who then fled."

"The postman banged on the window to check if Flint was alive," Sebastian said. "He said she was a dark-haired woman but didn't see her face. As Mrs Flint also has dark hair, Inspector Stone took those two descriptions as confirmation of her identity. And this time have sent her straight off to prison believing she murdered Micky White too. They're releasing Mr Sheringham."

"Mrs Flint has a solid alibi. She was at Millar's Hotel all morning," I said.

"It depends whether Stone is going to listen Norma, though," Lottie said.

"Hopefully a jury will," I said with a shudder. "If it comes to that. It's so dreadful. As soon as Mr Flint is home from the hospital, we'll have to interview him. There's something that's not sitting well with me." My head was beginning to thud. "Do you all mind if I take Prince out? I'm feeling a little overwrought and need half an hour to myself."

"Of course, Ellen," Hamilton said.

"We can update the notebook whilst you're out," Sebastian said.

"Yes," Lottie agreed. "There's so much to add to it."

. . .

BEFORE I LEFT THE HOTEL, I updated Angus Scott on my discovery that Violet had lost an emerald bracelet and asked him to ensure it was kept in the safe until we could clarify the position with her.

I walked along Beach Road in the opposite direction to the route I usually took. On my right was the fairground, and I passed this until I reached a more residential stretch of buildings on my left. Prince was not tugging at his leash and kept close by my side. I assumed that he sensed the tension I felt and I stroked his head intermittently to reassure him. Alone, I found it difficult to keep the tears from my eyes with the vision of Mrs Flint having been treated like a criminal imprinted on my mind. I could not imagine what she was feeling at that moment, being locked up in prison.

I reached the entrance of a large property to find Violet Sheringham staring at me.

"Are you well?" she asked. "I've received a call to ask me to collect Richard. They're releasing him and suggested I drove."

Tears continued to run down my face and I could see the shock in her face; this was not how a 'lady' acted, I knew that. I was supposed to keep a level of decorum. Even when I'd been delivered the news of my husband's death, I'd managed to remain composed until I was left alone. And now I was crying in the street over a woman I'd only known for little over four months and who was very much alive. *What is happening to me?* I asked myself.

"Do you wish to come up?" Violet asked. "Your make-up requires fixing."

I nodded and imagined the kohl would be smudged around my eyes. I certainly needed to make myself presentable before returning to The Grand.

"I heard they have arrested your friend, again," she said.

"Yes, it's so incredibly sad. I can't eradicate the image of her being led away."

"Did she do it?" Violet asked quietly.

"No, she even has a solid alibi. Unfortunately, Inspector Stone is a law unto himself."

"If anyone can find out what really happened, I'm sure you can," Violet said.

We covered the marble floor of the entrance hall. The walls were panelled in dark wood. It was nice to see it had been kept in its original style, rather than ripped out or painted in a modern fashion. We stepped into the lift, and the doorman pulled its iron cage doors which creaked as they shut. When the lift shuddered to a stop at the fourth floor, we stepped out. The hallway was lined with mahogany doors and the Sheringhams' flat was at the end.

Once inside, Violet left her handbag on a modern sofa. "I'll fix you a drink."

I was struck by the contrast between the Victorian grandeur of the building and the modernity of Violet's flat. The walls were a pale grey, hung with a few pieces of modern art. I caught my reflection in a stylish mirror, which confirmed that I indeed needed to fix my make-up.

Violet handed me a glass of brandy and pointed to the sofa. "Take a seat." It was upholstered in an emerald velvet, reminding me of the bracelet Violet had lost.

"Thank you," I said as I took a sip of the brandy. The air smelled of Violet's menthol cigarettes, one of which she was lighting as she sat on the sofa opposite me.

"Thank you for bringing me here," I said. "I've actually some news which may please you."

She frowned. "And what's that?"

"Your emerald bracelet. I believe it has been recovered. You will of course have to identify it but I found a bracelet in Micky's room."

She widened her blue eyes. "Really? I thought I'd left it with him. I asked him if he had it."

"You were in his room?" I asked.

She stood up and turned her back to me. "I don't want my husband to find out. It was a reckless moment." She spun around. "I'm young and I simply wanted to have a wild time. I know it's no excuse, but everyone seems to be having such fun these days..." She trailed off. "But the bracelet belonged to Richard's grandmother. I thought with there being a thief at The Grand that maybe the thief had stolen it after finding it at the hotel. I was suspicious when Michel, or should I say Micky, suddenly said he could afford the fare to America. The bracelet is worth more than enough to pay for a transatlantic ticket. I haven't been able to wear green since, as I always wear the bracelet when in green. Richard has already asked for me to wear it." She breathed out. "I'm so pleased you've located it."

I asked her to describe the item of jewellery and was completely convinced it was the same one. I would of course have to tell Rose that it was stolen. But if the woman was indeed coming into an insurance pay out, I did not feel as sorry for her. She didn't need to know that Violet was with Micky, but it would explain the dark hair on his pillow. Although, it was also entirely possible that a man such as Micky White could have entertained various brunettes in his bedroom.

"Would you like to come with me to The Grand to collect it before your husband returns?" I asked.

"Yes please," she said in a quiet voice. "I'll show you to my boudoir so you may fix your appearance."

"I won't mention the indiscretion to anyone," I said. I saw no reason to ruin the marriage which Violet clearly was making efforts to patch up.

"Thank you, I'd hate for Richard to know. I think deep down he suspects but...he'd be heartbroken. He's so stressed, he knew something was the matter with me. It's because I lost the bracelet and was worried he would find out." She gave a short laugh. "Turned out Richard thought that the reason I was stressed was that I'd strangled Michel." She looked at me her eyes glistening. "And yet he still loves me. He'd do anything for me, even take the blame for murder. I'll never find another man like Richard."

. . .

AFTER COLLECTING Violet's bracelet at the hotel, I spent time relaxing in my suite. Lottie and I agreed to meet Hamilton and Sebastian for a pre-dinner drink. The four of us were seated in the bar with the Simpson sisters. Major Fitzwilliam had not made it as he was having his meal in his room due to tiredness. Nelly was convinced an illness was making its way around the hotel and I wondered whether that was why I too had felt a little drained.

"I don't care what they say, she didn't do it!" Lottie said as we turned our discussions to Mrs Flint.

"I don't think she's guilty either," Nelly said. "Doesn't she have an alibi?"

"She was seen at Millar's Hotel, but it's only about one hundred yards from her house," I said. "It may have been feasible for her to pop out for ten minutes."

"She's clearly innocent," Hamilton said.

"We need to find a link between the two incidents." I lifted my glass and took a sip.

"Ryan said Stone was looking into other stranglings in the locations where Mrs Flint has visited when watching Joe in his shows."

"Oh my goodness," I said. "The Inspector is obsessed with those committing multiple murders."

"She's been to a show in Eastbourne where another strangling occurred," Sebastian said. "But PC Ryan said it happened well before Joe left town. As you say, Stone's fixated on repeat murders."

"Like the Vigilante Slasher," Betty said.

"The man is certainly obsessed with the Slasher, I'm

surprised he's still here, instead of London," Hamilton said. "It affects his judgement thinking all killers have multiple victims."

"But what if in this case, he was right?" I said. "That there is a link between Micky's murder, the attempt on Mr Flint's life."

"Mrs Flint is a link," Hamilton said with a sigh. "But I cannot accept it."

"We know it's not her," Nelly added.

"Well, it seems they've been unfaithful to their wives," Lottie said.

"Hell hath no fury like a woman scorned," Sebastian added.

"We have the continual reference to a dark-haired woman," I said.

"Douglas Flint is going to be sitting pretty if the police continue to think Ina did do it," Lottie said. "With the money Ina inherited sitting in their joint account."

"Two thousand pounds is a tidy sum," Hamilton added.

"He'll come out of it smelling like a bunch of roses," Lottie said. "And all the sympathy from the people who think Ina tried to kill him," she added as she sat up straight. "We must prove her innocence."

I spotted Rose White approaching Eddie at the bar.

"I need to speak to Mrs White," I said, wanting to inform her about the bracelet. "Would anyone care for more drinks?" They all nodded.

As I reached the bar, I asked another waiter to take

the orders at the table as Eddie was in conversation with Rose. When they noticed me, they stopped talking.

"I heard the news," Rose said. "It's a complete shock."

"I'm sure you realise that I'm not of the opinion that Mrs Flint killed Micky White or attempted to murder her husband. It would not have been easy to identify someone strangling you from behind. Mr Flint is likely mistaken and the postman merely pointed out that he saw a woman with dark hair." I looked at Rose's hair with an obvious glance.

"What you trying to say?" she said.

Eddie moved away to serve another hotel guest.

"Tell me again about the woman you met and went to Jake's Jazz bar with," I said. If I was able to locate the woman, it would verify her alibi.

"Oh her." She gestured out of the bar. "I saw her yesterday, when I went to The Branden Arms. The pub. It's so much more like home in there than this place."

"Are you sure?" I asked.

"Yeah. I said hello and she looked away as if she'd never met me before. But I knew it was her."

"Was she on her own?" I asked.

"No, she was talking to a man. Good looking bloke. Dark hair with flecks of grey and a dimple right in the middle of his chin."

Rose had perfectly described Douglas Flint.

"Really handsome," she added.

"And what about the woman he was with? Did you notice anything more about her appearance?"

"Not really. She's about forty with dark hair."

I quickly broke the news to Rose that the emerald bracelet had been claimed by another hotel guest, but was not concentrating on the conversation. I could not get out of my mind the picture of Douglas Flint in The Branden Arms with the woman who had taken Rose to Jake's Jazz bar then disappeared, just before Micky White had been strangled. I went back to re-join the others at the table, my mind feeling jumbled.

"Who on earth would kill Douglas Flint?" Lottie said as I sat down.

"He's not dead though, is he?" I said in a slow voice. "Lottie, when Norma Lloyd made reference to Douglas Flint having had an affair with a Mabel, do you know who the woman was?"

"Mabel Kerr, the one who owns The Branden Arms," she said.

Various things were fitting into place, although my mind still felt clouded with some details that didn't quite fit. I needed to sort them before I came to a conclusion. "It's often easier to piece the information together at the scene of the crime," I said quietly. "Let's meet in the ballroom."

"Can we come?" Betty asked eagerly.

I smiled. "Of course! But give me a quarter of an hour to myself, to mull it over." I knew I was close.

CHAPTER 21

*I*nside the ballroom with the notebook in hand, I stood in the middle of the dance floor and slowly rotated, taking in the entire room, including the various entrances and exits – those where someone with murder in mind could potentially enter and leave without being spotted. It was quiet and eerie, and as the scene of the crime came into view, I imagined the strangled Micky White at my feet and gulped.

A door opened and I jumped.

Eddie walked in with a large box in his arms, jangling with what I assumed were bottles of drinks. "We don't open for another two hours," he said.

"I'm simply thinking," I replied.

"Looking for clues?" he asked with a sarcastic laugh. "The police are convinced that woman from Millar's Hotel done it. Especially since she tried to top her husband. There's been so much death up there, I doubt they'll ever reopen that place."

"Mrs Flint is innocent," I said in a clear voice.

As Eddie placed the box on the bar, it clanged. "If you say so." He approached me then stood by my side and lowered his voice staring at the place where Micky had lain. "I weren't keen on the bloke, but seeing his dead body was sobering."

"I didn't realise you saw his body?" I said.

"Yeah." He paused for a while as if lost in thought. "I came in with Mr Scott when the doctor arrived." He stepped away from me. "I've not been the same since it happened. I smile at people, I make conversation, but I can't get rid of the sight of him." He approached the bar then turned around. "Out of respect I've not drunk a drop of alcohol since. I don't think I can face the mood of a hangover, not with the pictures I see in my mind." Eddie ran a hand through his hair. "Micky's eyes were staring up at me." He appeared to shudder. "We didn't always see eye-to-eye but he helped me out a lot. Even if I did end up owing him. And yeah, I said a couple of times I'd expose him, but that was just to buy time to pay him back. Micky was my connection to London." He paused. "Since he's been gone, I've been feeling homesick. Anyway, I've more bottles to collect."

He swaggered away, his confident steps juxtaposed with the vulnerability he'd displayed. I listened to the sound of his footsteps in the quiet ballroom until the door banged shut behind him. Alone I felt a nervous tremble and followed the direction Eddie had taken, but as I reached the door it opened. Blocking my exit was the bulk of Herbert Lightfoot.

"You're snooping around again, are you?" he said with a slow shake of his head.

"If you would excuse me, Mr Lightfoot, I need to attend to my dog."

He stood to one side. "When the police asked me who I thought the hotel thief was, I told them it might be you!"

I stopped in my tracks. "Don't be ridiculous!"

"It's the ideal cover, a lady of the realm, hankering after a bit of excitement, poking your nose it where it don't belong. Why not have the extra thrill of theft? What is it you're searching for here – in Branden Bay?"

I was momentarily stunned by his words and found I could not find an answer to them. "They've caught the culprit," I said.

"Yeah, I know. I was surprised at young Fred. I liked him."

"A man?" I asked.

"Not much more than a lad." He grinned at me. "Didn't the great detective know?"

I'd actually expected it had been a woman with long dark hair, but I did not say that. I felt myself tremble a little.

"Fred looks like butter wouldn't melt in his mouth, with his angelic golden hair." He looked me up and down. "Looks can be deceiving."

"Yes, they certainly are," I said as a trickle of realisation set in, I gulped. *Surely not!* I thought. I knew I must return to my suite immediately. "If you will excuse me." I passed the man and headed towards the reception.

I took the stairs, rather than waiting for the lift and panted as I reached the third floor, the nerves I experienced were affecting my breathing. After passing the lifts, the door to the Simpson sisters' room opened.

"Oh, you made me jump," I said with a nervous laugh.

"We were just coming down to the ballroom to see you!" Betty said grinning at me with the smile I'd felt warm me on many occasions over the previous weeks.

"Have you changed your mind?" Nelly asked me with a frown.

"It was unnerving in the deserted ballroom alone, I came up to talk it through with everyone," I said. "Would you care to join me?"

"Nelly has a theory," Betty added. "I thought she must be wrong, but when she explained it...my lady, it makes perfect sense. Please come in and hear what she has to say before we tell the others." Betty appeared so excited. "To see what you think. It would be so thrilling for us to have cracked it!"

I felt a pang of sadness realising how it was possible to be so completely duped by others. How those closest to us, can let us down. And no other could feel so betrayed as Mrs Flint. I knew deep down, if I talked it through with the sisters, I would most certainly get to the bottom of the matter – still it would be more sensible to do so with those waiting in my suite.

"Come on," Betty said with a smile that was so

warm it could have melted ice. There was something so caring and charming about her, that was quite hard to resist.

"She took my arm. "Please."

"Would you like a sherry?" Nelly asked as we stepped inside their room.

"No thank you," I said. "I need my mind to be clear."

"Take a seat, tell us where your thoughts are, dear," Betty said gesturing to the chair at their dressing table. "Then Nelly can tell you her theory."

I pulled the chair out and sat down as the sisters plonked themselves on the closest bed. I looked at Betty smiling at me, and then to Nelly who sat with her hands on her lap and her back ramrod straight.

"You have to look at who has the most to gain," Nelly said with a satisfied sniff emulating a school governess. "You could start there."

"A few people gained from Micky White's death," I said. "Firstly, his wife, Rose. She's been released from a marriage to a man who was unfaithful for years and had stopped sending her the money needed to care for their family. She will now benefit from a life insurance policy, the existence of which she failed to mention to us. Then we have Herbert Lightfoot, he gained his job back having previously lost everything, dance means so much to him as well as the financial benefits which come with the position here at The Grand. Then, there are the Sheringhams, they both had issues with Micky. Violet had let slip details of her past and Micky was threatening to tell everyone and embarrass her and

Richard Sheringham is no fool, he realised Violet's friendship with Micky was a threat to their marriage. They've both strengthened their position with Micky gone. And finally, Eddie, who's had his loan effectively written off with Micky no longer able to demand repayment."

Nelly and Betty exchanged a satisfied glance, but I knew their theory involved someone who was not on the list of suspects written in the notebook, which I now held on my lap.

"However," I said. "Someone else benefited from Micky White's death, but only if Mrs Flint took the blame." I shook my head. "But to believe that the husband of Mrs Flint wanted her to take the blame for the death so he could keep her inheritance leaves me with a heavy heart."

Betty bit her lip and her smile faded. "Yes, I know it's awful for your friend."

"She should know what sort of man her husband is!" Nelly said. "What kind of man feel's happy that his wife is to be sent to the gallows, so he'll have control of her money. There's only one punishment he should endure."

"A terrible man," Betty said with a slow shake of her head. The lightness now devoid from her eyes. "He deserves to be hung."

I nodded. "It's sickening. When Mrs Flint told me that she'd placed the funds she'd inherited in a joint account, I thought it unwise, but later began to wonder whether something more sinister was afoot."

"He was unfaithful to his wife," Nelly said, "with that woman from the pub. It was her that probably did it. He must have found out somehow, that Mrs Flint was going to have dance lessons and cooked the plan up with his mistress."

"The evidence is compelling," I said. "When I visited the Flint home with Captain Hamilton a woman came out, we only saw her from the back, but she had dark hair. Mr Flint told us it was his cleaner. Yet, his house was dirty. Surely a cleaner would have tidied the place?"

"So it was Mrs Kerr in the house and not a cleaner?" Nelly said. "He was probably in her arms while his poor wife was in the cells!"

"The man is despicable," Betty said. "He needs to pay!"

"Yes," I said. "The fact is, Douglas Flint had been rekindling his affair with Mabel Kerr and I feel awful at the prospect of having to reveal that to Ina." I shook my head. "She has had so much to deal with, I can't imagine what it's like in prison." I forced a smile. "But at least she'll soon be released."

"An awful man," Nelly said with much force.

"Exactly," I said. "And when Mrs Flint was at the police station, her husband made no effort to visit her, and only sent her a letter saying how upset *he* felt. He was giving the police the impression that he thought his wife was more than capable of murder."

"What sort of woman is this Mabel Kerr?" Betty asked me.

"Mrs Kerr's husband died and following this, a local gangster used to rent a room from her pub, he left a roulette table and she's running an illegal gambling business from The Branden Arms, no doubt with the help of Mr Flint who seems unable to visit his wife in the cells but more than capable of spending long nights in the pub. Mabel Kerr is not a woman who plays by the rules."

"So, she was the woman Rose White met here, at the hotel," Betty said excitedly. "And then took Rose to Jake's Jazz Bar, maybe to get her out of the way in case she returned to the ballroom. Then Mrs Kerr disappeared, went back to The Grand and strangled Micky White!"

"Rose White will have to identify the woman," I said slowly. "Before she leaves for London."

Nelly frowned and exchanged a look with Betty.

"There was something I didn't understand," Betty said quickly. "Why would Mrs Kerr try to kill Douglas Flint with all the money he's got in the bank?" She looked back to me. "It didn't make sense." She turned to her sister with a smile. "Then Nelly had her theory."

I thought I would let them have their say. I knew Nelly was itching to deliver her verdict.

"The whole point is that he's not dead," Nelly added with a satisfied smile. "The strangler never intended for Mr Flint to die."

"They waited for the postman," Betty added. "Before putting the scarf around his neck. With Mrs Kerr's face obscured so all he could see was the colour of her hair, she pulled the scarf tight to mark Mr Flint's neck as he struggled. Then as soon as the postman spotted her, she fled."

"And MR Flint identified her as his wife," Nelly said. "He framed Ina, and even if the police still can't pin Mickey's death on her, they'll get her for attempted murder of her husband."

This whole situation had of course occurred to me. "In this scenario," I said. "You believe that Douglas Flint and Mrs Kerr cooked up the whole murder of Micky White with the sole aim of framing Ina Flint."

"Yes, so she would go to prison for the rest of her life or worse, get the death penalty. They'd be free to spend all her money!" Betty said. "But I'd hate for Mrs Flint to take the blame," Betty added with what I imagined was complete sincerity.

"Mr Flint and Mrs Kerr should pay for their indiscretions," Nelly said in a stern voice.

I stood up, my mouth was dry. "Well done ladies, you are indeed super sleuths."

"And you had the same thought?" Betty asked her eyebrows raised.

"Indeed. It certainly clouded my judgement," I said without thinking.

Nelly narrowed her eyes at me.

I caught her gaze and it was as if she could see straight into my mind and read it. I gulped. Acting was never my forte, Phoebe had often remarked that I was an open book and we often found ourselves caught out by the dormitory mistress simply by the expression of guilt on my face. My left eye twitched.

Nelly glanced at Betty and the sisters' eyes darted to each other and then back at me.

I gave a short, nervous laugh. "I'd better be off then." I gestured to the door. "Are you coming?" My palms felt so hot that my notebook had become stuck to my skin as I clutched it in my right hand.

Nelly walked swiftly to the door and locked it. Then turned and stared at me.

Oh no, I thought. I'd played with fire. I could see it in their eyes. I was in serious trouble.

CHAPTER 22

I remained silent as Betty and Nelly continued to stare at me.

"I think you're hiding something," Betty said. The usual sparkle in her eyes was now absent.

"Why don't you sit down and tell us what you really think?" Nelly said and popped the door key into the pocket of her skirt.

"Do as Nelly says." Betty's voice sounded somewhat different, losing its soft nature and was devoid of frailty.

I remained calm, considering what options were available to me, to extract myself from this situation. *Shall I scream?* I thought. It was unlikely I would be heard by the others in my suite. It was ten doors down the corridor and the walls were made of thick stone, not bricks. The thought of Lottie, Hamilton, Sebastian and my darling Prince suddenly instigated a fleeting panic. *Hold it together*, I told myself as I took a deep breath and counted to three in my head before taking a seat.

"Go on," Nelly said. "Tell us what you think you know!"

I began: "Mr Flint's clear desire for his wife to be guilty so he could spend her money and explore his extramarital affair with Mrs Kerr clouded my judgment. They are facts that cannot be disputed. He clearly wants his wife to be guilty whether she is or not. He has a motive for Ina to be charged with murder. He is undoubtedly guilty of being a thoroughly poor husband, but that does not mean that he murdered Micky White and framed his wife for it."

"You're just like us," Betty nodded. "That's why you knew. You understand what we've done and what we have to do!"

"And now you're too far in," Nelly said. "It's your own fault of course. You should have minded your own business."

"It was made my business," I said calmly. "I've been helping a friend clear her name. But I'd dispute your assertion that we are alike!"

"We know you killed Major Coltrane," Betty scoffed.

"We don't judge you for your actions," Nelly added. "Far from it. We applaud you. He was dishonest and unfaithful when you were engaged to him years ago."

"I did not kill Major Albert Coltrane," I said. He'd died when I'd first arrived in Branden Bay and it was certainly not by my hand. It had been reported in the newspaper.

"You covered it up well," Betty said ignoring my words. "We admired you for it. Us three, we're alike. It's a shame, we really do like you. If there was a way?" She turned to her sister.

"There is no way," Nelly said with a huff.

I looked across to the window, but noticed there was no balcony, unlike my suite. It was not somewhere I could easily escape from. I decided I would need to keep them talking, hoping that there was a better window in the bathroom.

"When did you realise?" Betty asked me.

I gestured to her. "Your real name is Juliet, the wife of the late Mr Taverham of Taverham Shoes. I saw your passport at the police station. The thief took it when they stole your ring. Your hand hesitated over it. I thought you were being curious, as was I, due to our investigation. I guess you were wondering whether you could take it without anyone noticing."

Betty's sickly smile slipped from her face and her expression changed.

"Lottie was right," I continued. "The link between the victims of strangulation was that all of the men had committed adultery."

"Luke made my sister's life a living hell," Nelly said. "He deserved everything he got."

"Mrs Taverham here is not convinced, though, are you?" I said looking at the woman I had come to know as Betty. "You miss your husband and I presume it's your own ring you wear around your neck and the tears you shed when it was stolen — were genuine."

"Keep Luke out of this." Betty bit her lip.

"She told me, when she'd had too many drinks, that Luke died thinking she had no love for him. Well, he certainly would have thought that if she'd strangled him to death, with your help." I gestured at Nelly. "You may well be comfortable with it, but Betty has regrets."

"She does not!" Nelly shouted at me. I thought my only hope was to create a disagreement between the sisters.

"I guess you both framed his mistress who is now in prison." I stood up.

"She deserves the gallows," Betty said. "She stole my Luke and if she didn't do that, he'd still be alive today. She's to blame for his death not us!"

The sisters exchanged glances, clearly my attempt at dividing them had failed.

"Don't upset yourself, Betty," Nelly said. "You did the night thing. We both know that."

Whilst they were distracted, I took a small sideways step towards the bathroom. "You were close to Eddie," I said to Betty. "No doubt plying him with drinks then asking him all about the ballroom and the various exits and entrances, making it easy to slip into the ballroom and strangle Micky. Was he even in the ballroom when you arrived?"

"Micky was already in our sights, but after the awful things his wife told my sister, we decided he had to be punished there and then. So I went to his room,"

Betty said. "And asked him for a late lesson so I could dance with Major Fitzwilliam. He was tired but I offered to pay him double."

"I bet you couldn't believe your luck when you found Mrs Flint's scarf in there and didn't have to use one of your own!" I said.

"I was dancing with him, and Nelly came from the curtain and grabbed him from behind."

"It was quick," Nelly said. "But the world is a better place without Micky White."

The sisters stood side by side both with half smiles upon their faces. I had seen them as two sweet older women, how wrong I'd been. They took a step towards me and I knew I would need to continue talking. They clearly loved the feeling of significance that murder had given them; I could see it in their eyes.

"You were both rather complimentary of the Vigilante Slasher," I said. "Is that how you see yourselves? Vigilantes? Doing women a favour by ridding the world of unfaithful husbands? I take it you also killed the man in Eastbourne?"

Betty glanced at Nelly then back at me. "Considering you will not be telling anyone, yes. That was Nelly."

"We need to finish this," Nelly said. "And quick. We're taking too many chances."

"I presume you sold Taverham Shoes?" I added, hoping to play for time as I yet again moved one step closer to the bathroom. "You must be incredibly rich."

"We both worked hard at that business while Luke

was off with his mistress," Nelly said. "We deserved it. We'd have had nothing if Betty divorced him, no matter the change in the law, women may well be able to divorce their husbands but what's the point when you're left penniless and homeless? Get the scarf," Nelly said to her sister.

"I must compliment you, though," I said and was relieved when Betty stopped before she reached the wardrobe and turned towards me. "How did you find out where Douglas Flint lived?"

"Nelly met him in The Branden Arms the night before, to check we had the same man." Betty grinned. "Then followed him home."

"He loved himself. I wish I'd finished him off," Nelly said.

"You arranged the perfect alibi for Mr Flint's planned death," I said. "By bringing me here to make it look as if you, Nelly were asleep in front of the fire, thus giving you both an alibi. With Nelly asleep and Betty at the police station who would have thought either of you were responsible for Mr Flint's death, had you have been successful and not been interrupted by the postman!" I peered at Nelly. "I wondered why your hair was always so perfectly styled. It's clear now that it's a wig." I gestured to Betty. "You're both wearing wigs. You drugged Major Fitzwilliam and left him in the chair with Nelly's wig on. Taking me to his room to pretend to ask him to join us." I'd realised when piecing the information together that the dark hair I'd found on the dressing table belonged to one of the sisters.

"I told you she's clever," Betty said to her sister then smiled at me. "But not clever enough."

Nelly pulled off her wig to reveal her long day hair and then opened the wardrobe, removing a scarf.

"I'm not saying I'm clever," I said, trying to keep a steady voice even though at this stage my knees were trembling as Betty also removed her wig. She better resembled the picture I'd seen of Juliet Taverham in her passport.

"It's lucky that Mr Flint is such an evil man that he falsely identified his wife, and not me as the killer!" Nelly said with a laugh.

"True, Mr Flint muddied the waters," I said. "But it was not that which gave it away."

Nelly stopped in her tracks, allowing me to take one more pace towards the bathroom. "What do you mean?" she asked.

"Betty said that Eddie had told you both that Micky was married and unfaithful to his wife," I said. "But Eddie said he's not drunk since Micky's death, so I knew he told you that information before Micky died. You knew he was an adulterer, that he was from London and this was confirmed when you bumped into his wife, in the hotel reception."

"I told you not to mention Micky's history," Nelly said to her sister.

"I wanted to make it look as if we were really inter-ested in solving the case!" Betty said in her defence.

Nelly gestured at me. "You handed that one to her, lucky she was stupid enough to walk in here!" She approached me, wrapping each end of the scarf in her hands.

I took this as my only opportunity to escape and thrust open the bathroom door then slammed it shut, my hands shook as I swiftly pulled the lock across. I turned around, taking deep breaths as I leaned on the closed door, trying to block Nelly's shouts and thumps on the wood from my mind. I had to concentrate and call for help. I hurried to the sash window and lifted the lower part and looked out, there was only a tiny ledge.

"Help," I called out, but the tide was coming in and the accompanying wind whipped my voice away.

I heard the door behind me splinter as the women hit it. With my heart thudding, I knew I had no option but to to climb out of the window. I gingerly lifted my leg over the windowsill feeling the weather blowing around my stockinged legs. I stepped onto the slim ledge, trembling as the strong sea wind blew across my body. I inched along the small space available to me, away from the window, wondering whether I was about to take my final steps. Keeping my gaze straight, I took a deep breath then lowered my eyes to passers-by, who appeared small from the third floor.

I breathed in and placed my back to the wall. "Help," I called out as loud as I could. "Help."

I heard a woman scream and as I lowered my eyes again, spotted a couple of people rush towards the building, hopefully heading inside to call the police. I looked straight ahead again, because I felt dizzy each time I glanced downwards. I heard the thuds on the bathroom door, telling me that the sisters had still not broken through. I lowered my chin to chest so I could get a better perspective. Although it was limited, it was with relief that I spotted the flaming red hair of Angus Scott. I lifted my head again, knowing he would know exactly which room I was outside. I looked to my right to suddenly see the dark hair of Betty appear.

She looked down at the small crowd forming below. "Ruth," she called out to her sister. "We need to go!"

I wasn't quite sure how long I remained there, chanting to myself to remain calm. I knew that it would only take one falter or slip and I would surely fall to my death. *What will become of Ashcombe Hall if I die?* I asked myself. *Will it be split up and sold off in pieces?*

I felt as if I'd been on the ledge for ages, although it was likely only a matter of minutes. I looked down again, chin to chest, and saw them — two dark-haired women running towards a motorbus with cases. One plump, one slim. Mrs Juliet Taverham was escaping with her sister and there was nothing I could do about it.

I heard Lottie's voice beside me as she leaned out of the window. "Ellen, what happened?"

"Don't come out," I shouted. "I don't want to risk you or anyone else falling."

"Ellen, stay still," Hamilton said. "The fire brigade has been called."

My legs wobbled as rain began to fall, lashing against my face with the gusts coming in from the sea. I wanted to find my voice to tell Hamilton how I felt about him. It may well have been different to the love I'd felt for Leonard, but that did not make it less real. I swayed a little, overcome by a bout of dizziness before I felt a strong arm across my chest.

"Hold on, Ellen," Hamilton shouted to me through the stormy weather.

The bell of the fire engine reached my ears and I shut my eyes, concentrating on Hamilton's strong arm, until I heard the clank of the ladder and the welcomed sturdy arms of the fireman. I wept with relief as he helped me to safety, guiding me back to the window.

I SPENT hours at the police station, enduring Inspector Stone's questions as I made a statement, explaining exactly what had happened, with Hamilton by my side.

"You let the murderers get away?" Stone asked me.

"Look here, man," Hamilton said. "Lady Ellen has solved this mystery, it's not her job to apprehend the killers."

"It's not her job to poke her nose in, either," Stone said. "And keep valuable information from the police."

"My only involvement was to stop the wrongful arrest of Mrs Flint. Now, if you would apply for her release from prison, I shall prepare for my return to Ashcombe Hall at the earliest convenience! My trip to Branden Bay has been far from the relaxing trip I'd hoped for." I stifled a yawn.

"You would do better in future to listen to Lady

Ellen," Hamilton said. "Before incarcerating innocent citizens."

Inspector Stone narrowed his eyes at Hamilton. "I hear you were in London recently."

"That's correct I have a client there," Hamilton replied.

Stone stared at him silently for at least five seconds. "We sir, have unfinished business," he growled.

"What's that supposed to imply?" Hamilton said to him in a cool and measured tone. It was akin to viewing two men about to box.

Stone continued to stare at him then moved his attention to me. "Do not involve yourself in any more crimes. You nearly died at the hands of a pair of deranged women and we will need to ensure you have adequate security until we apprehend them."

"I can assure you, Inspector, I wish for a peaceful life," I said. "But before I leave, I think I know where Mrs Taverham and her sister are headed to." I had thought back to the last time Betty had been drinking too much alcohol.

Stone raised his pen. "Yes?"

"I think they've gone south — to Torquay."

CHAPTER 23

"*P*hoebe, it's so good to hear your voice," I said into the telephone receiver in Angus Scott's office.

"Are you back at the hall?" she asked.

"No, I'll be there Saturday. I'm still at The Grand Hotel. I've so much news to tell you." I proceeded to give my closest friend the details of events since I'd last seen her at Denham Hall. She gasped in certain places and I had to admit that I enjoyed relaying the story to her.

"Has Inspector Stone set off to Torquay to find the Taverham woman and her sister?" she asked.

"Yes, and I do hope he finds them, otherwise he'll think I sent him on a wild goose chase. But it appears the sisters have killed a few unfaithful men in various towns they have visited."

"I can't wait to tell Alex." Phoebe's husband was best friends with Alexander, the Duke of Loxborough, who appeared to have an affection for me, but who I found thoroughly annoying. "He asks after you every time I see him and he's popping in here on his way south, having been on business in London. I always thought you two would be a super pairing."

"Phoebe, there's something particular I wanted to discuss with you." I hesitated.

"Ah, is it about your Captain Hamilton?" she asked.

"Yes," I said with a laugh. "He's leaving this evening for Bristol on the last train and then travelling south. In a few days he'll be sailing to Cairo from Plymouth and will be gone for many weeks. I'm worried that if I don't tell him explicitly that I've much affection for him, he may strike up a friendship elsewhere."

"From what I gathered from Lottie when you were here, the man is besotted with you, so I doubt that will be the case. However, there's nothing wrong with letting the fellow know how you feel. Are you bothered by what society will think?"

"I would say no, but then I'm so aware of the position that Lottie and Lord Garthorn are in. Deep down maybe I do judge my own situation."

"Ellen, you deserve to be happy. Now, give the man a kiss goodbye that he won't forget," she said with a laugh.

"Phoebe, really!" I laughed.

"Yes, really. Anyway, Alex will be here very soon, but I'll drive over to Ashcombe on Wednesday to see you."

I felt happier having spoken to Phoebe. She always

made me feel better, during all sorts of calamities in my life, starting from when we were at boarding school together. She was the person who made me feel that anything was possible. As I replaced the receiver, Mr and Mrs Scott arrived in the office.

"It's lovely to see you, my lady," Dora Scott said. She looked so much healthier than when I'd seen her previously. There was colour in her cheeks and her white hair had been cut, framing her face. She had clearly allowed the sun to kiss her skin whilst she had been away. The last time I saw her, she was so pale and frail I had nearly mistaken her for a ghost. She now looked a lot more like a healthy young woman.

I stood up and walked around the desk to greet her. "Welcome home."

She put her hands together as if in prayer. "I have to thank you so much for your kindness and generosity, providing me with the right care for my...nerves." She lowered her voice. "And for sorting out the unfortunate issue with the dancer."

"It's no problem at all," I said, but at the same time felt somewhat weary.

"I understand you're returning to the hall this weekend?"

"Yes, I am."

"We do not want any payment for your stay here," Angus said and placed an arm around his wife.

"There's no need," I said.

"We realise that, but we want to cover your costs." They both smiled at me with so much thanks that I suddenly felt my trip to Branden Bay had been worth it.

I FELT extreme butterflies as I dressed for the last evening I was to spend with Hamilton before his extended trip. My hands trembled as I attempted to style my hair.

"Let me do that for you, Ellen," Lottie said gently. She took the pomade and smoothed my hair into waves. Even though I had shunned assistance for months, it felt relaxing simply to submit and allow her to help. "Are you upset about saying goodbye to Ernest?" Lottie asked.

"I am, yes," I said then felt the need to justify my answer. "It's not surprising, since we've spent so much time together over recent months."

"Ernest really loves you," Lottie said clearly ignoring my wish to diffuse the romantic connotations in her tone of voice. She caught my gaze via the mirror. "I don't know why you don't tell each other exactly how you feel."

I lowered my gaze. "We're not young like yourself and Sebastian."

"Sebastian gave me a ring," she said, showing me her right hand. He had received a letter from his parents, demanding his return to London, and had left early that morning. "He said I'll never have to doubt his love."

"It's beautiful," I said, looking at the sapphire ring

with a smile.

"He's going to visit us in Ashcombe," she said.

I lifted my gaze to see her face beaming at me via the reflection. I wished I could feel as confident of Hamilton's affection as Lottie was of Sebastian's.

As WE DESCENDED the stairs to the restaurant, Hamilton looked exceptionally dapper, as if he had visited the barber. He held his hand out for mine. I took it and he led me to the restaurant and to our table as Lottie followed us.

We enjoyed a light-hearted meal. Major Fitzwilliam had also joined us. I had thought the Major would be extremely glum, having lost the attention of who he had come to know as the Simpson sisters, however it transpired that he had been losing a fortune to them at cards every day. After I'd explained that Betty was actually a thirty-nine-year-old woman and not a lady in her late fifties, he had chuckled and said that his late wife would have called him a silly old goat. As much as I'd wished for a new love for the Major, it was clearly too soon for the man.

I glanced at the clock. Hamilton was due to leave town on the last train to Bristol at eleven.

"Would you care for a visit to the ballroom before I leave?" he asked me.

"I think that would be marvellous," I said, my heart beating a little faster.

As we entered the ballroom, Eddie approached us. "Well done Lady Ellen, the sisters had us all duped."

I looked to Lottie. "Lottie was upset, she was quite taken with Betty."

"I was until I realised that I just missed my own family," she said.

"That's how I feel," Eddie said. "I'm going back to London with Rose, straight after Micky's funeral. I'll probably stay there and maybe come back to Branden Bay in the summer."

"Ellen says that as soon as we're settled in at the hall, my family can come for a visit." Lottie beamed at me.

Once we had located a table, we sat down and the band played 'Fascination' by Fermo Dante Marchetti, reminding me that I had danced to the tune with Major Fitzwilliam. I smiled at the Major and then to Hamilton.

Hamilton stood up. "Would you honour me with this dance?" he asked.

As he took me to the floor, it was as if the rest of the room faded away. He held me close and looked into my eyes. We danced the whole piece, with no words spoken, however I felt so close to him, and not only in physical proximity. The music flowed through my body and I wondered whether this would be the last time I ever danced with him. A tear stung my eye as the music drew to a close.

"Are you well?" Hamilton asked with concern.

"I may be in need of a little fresh air," I said.

As we passed the table, I told Lottie and the Major that we were popping outside for some air. Lottie stood up and gave Hamilton a farewell embrace, it brought it home to me, that she was allowing us time alone to say our goodbye. I picked up my handbag and Hamilton guided me out and through the reception. It was there that I saw his bags, ready to be collected. I glanced at the clock which showed that we had but ten minutes left together. *You really have left this to the last minute,* I told myself as a lump formed in my throat, realising time was running out to express my feelings for him.

He led me outside, the night air was cool against my skin. "Ellen," he began, "these past few months, though clouded with death and theft, have been some of the most precious times of my life."

I tried to smile, but the ache in my chest grew. "I've treasured your company also," I said, though the words felt far too bland for what I truly felt inside.

He reached into his coat, pulling out a folded piece of paper. "I have an address for you," he said, holding it out. "I'm unsure as to how easily a letter will find its way to me, but the thought that you may write...well, it would give me something to look forward to."

As I took the paper, my fingers brushed against his. My heart thumped. *Tell him,* a voice inside me urged. *Tell him now.* "I'll miss you," I whispered, my eyes searching his, silently pleading for him to detect the emotion I felt inside.

He stepped closer and reached for my hand.

"It won't be the same without you," I said.

He leaned in. His lips brushed mine, gently. But the moment was fleeting. He pulled back as if startled by his own bold move and ran a hand over his hair. "Forgive me," he stammered and turned away as if expecting me to berate him.

I stepped forward and placed a hand on his back. He turned and I touched his arm and ran my hand down until I felt his hand within mine and smiled at him, unblinking.

He pressed his lips to mine again, this time with certainty and we shared the most beautiful kiss during which I felt so perfectly close to him in a place inhabited by only us two. After pulling away, the kiss left me rather dizzy.

He gazed down at me with a smile that matched my own. "You're the most beautiful woman I've ever known."

I held his gaze. "I'll be waiting for you and as well as posting a letter, I'll write others to save for your return."

A motorcar horn interrupted us and Hamilton squeezed my hand. "That's my transport to the station."

The car had been loaded with his luggage by the porter who I assume had witnessed our very public kiss. I smiled to myself, the old Ellen would never have kissed a man in public, not even the one I'd married.

"Goodbye, Ellen." Hamilton turned away.

I called after him. "Ernest!" I hurried to the car, pulling the envelope that I'd been carrying around with me for nearly two weeks from my handbag. "Something to read on the train." I grinned at him. "See you in a few weeks." I gave him another kiss, brief but bold, upon his lips.

He wrapped his arms around me again and squeezed me tight. "You're everything I could ever want."

Hamilton waved from the window as the car pulled away. I was filled with a nervous energy as I imagined him finally reading my letter. I had been left with the certainty that Captain Ernest Hamilton was falling in love with me.

CHAPTER 24

*P*rince barked excitedly as we neared
Ashcombe Hall. I knew he was desperate
to jump from the car and was pleased that I'd decided
to leave the roof in place, even if it was a sunny day.
Our luggage had been transported via train and
collected by my chauffeur, George in my other larger
car. However, I'd driven myself and Lottie home in my
less practical Rolls Royce. It was lovely to be on the
road again. We had said farewell to Mrs Lloyd, Mr
Breckon and Mrs Flint, who was now overcoming her
ordeal. Mrs Flint had not returned to her marital
home. With the money she'd inherited, she was considering purchasing a property. Norma and John Breckon
were still determined to seek alternative employment
and I said that I would ask around for any suitable
positions.

"Do you think they'll like me?" Lottie asked,
bringing me out of my thoughts.

"Who?"

"Your staff, Dawkins, your cook and butler?"

I laughed. "Of course they will." I looked across at her as she chewed on her lip. "Don't worry, I'll be keeping an eye on you and you'll have a bedroom close to mine, not above with the other staff or off site in the cottages."

"Won't people think I'm above my station? Like Mrs Flint used to say?"

"Lottie, you are above your station," I said with a laugh. "You're courting Lord Garthorn."

Lottie gave me a broad grin. "I guess you're right."

As we turned into the long drive, Lottie gasped. "Oh, my goodness. I've never seen such a big building. It's larger than Denham and Bandberry."

I stopped the car and looked ahead as my eyes misted over – the hall was like no other and as I sat in the car, looking at my lifelong home, something inside me shifted. The weight of responsibility of keeping this grand, sprawling estate appeared to melt away as I appreciated the beauty of the sandstone towers, with its windows glinting in the afternoon sun. It had always been my home and gazing at it in that moment, I felt the beating heart of my family, as if the hall itself was the last remaining member of the Ashcombe blood line. I knew then that I could not simply give it away. It was a part of me. I could never leave and would do my level best to protect Ashcombe, to ensure that if I passed without heir, that future generations would be able to appreciate its beauty.

Prince wined and I put my foot on the accelerator as he scrambled on the back seat, eager to get out. "Welcome to your new home, Lottie," I managed to say through my emotion.

As I approached the front of the building, I saw Dawkins, her long skirt billowing in the wind, and behind her someone pushing one of the old wheelchairs left over from the convalescent home. As I reached them, I saw it was my cook, pushing Johnson my butler. I stopped the car, aghast. They appeared so elderly.

I quickly exited the car and rushed to them, bursting into floods of tears as Prince ran wild in circles and then jumped up at my cook and then to Johnson who patted his head.

"Welcome home, Lady Ellen," Dawkins said.

I took her in my arms, her body stiff, as if she did not know how to react to this unexpected display of emotion. "I've missed you," I said. "And you've been so faithful to me, looking after the hall whilst I have been away gallivanting."

"You needed the rest, my lady," Dawkins said and gave my back a single pat.

I stepped back and looked at her and then at my cook. Both I realised must be well into their seventies, and Johnson – he'd outlived four earls. I would not have been surprised if he was in his nineties.

I took a deep breath. "You three have worked so hard. And I know you've objected in the past. But as from tomorrow, you will commence your pensions."

"We can't abandon you!" the cook said.

Johnson did not object and simply nodded.

"Who will you find to do our jobs?" Dawkins asked.

As Lottie reached me, I put my arm around her. "I know the perfect candidates."

By the following Wednesday, I'd completed a full inspection of the renovations and provided guidance on the finishing touches that had required approval. I was sitting in my drawing room, awaiting the arrival of Phoebe who was driving herself over from Denham Hall. Prince was asleep by my feet after a long walk on the estate. He was so much happier now that he was home. I welcomed being alone for a short while as it had been an extremely busy few days. Lottie had been quieter than usual, but understandably it would take her some time to adjust to her new life. She had kept herself busy setting up a new office for me. I'd called Mr Breckon, Mrs Lloyd and Mrs Flint to invite them to Ashcombe Hall to discuss my proposition of employment. However, they had pressed me for the details, and all had agreed, without knowing any of the terms, to take up employment in Ashcombe Hall. I had wondered whether Mrs Flint would agree, considering she could have potentially retired on her inheritance which she'd successfully removed from the joint account she'd held with her husband. But she was extremely eager on the caveat that she was allowed enough leave, to visit some of her son's shows. The three were working a fortnight's notice at Millar's Hotel and helping the owners recruit replacements.

There was a knock on the door and Lottie entered.

"How are you getting along?" I asked her.

"I've opened all today's post for you, but there was this package. It's marked confidential, so I thought you should open it yourself."

I frowned as I looked at the small parcel.

"Shall I leave you to open it in private?" she asked.

"No, stay," I said, feeling as if I wanted her with me. I undid the string tied around the brown paper which covered the package. Once unwrapped the parcel revealed an oblong box. I lifted the lid and felt a burst of nausea. Inside was one pair of gold-rimmed glasses with diamanté detail.

Lottie put a hand to her throat "They look like Betty's glasses," she whispered. "Although, her name's really Juliet. Why has she sent them to you? Do you think it's threat that she knows where you are?"

"They could be her sister's," I said as I pulled out the accompanying note which fluttered in my hand as I held it. I read the note in silence as Lottie did the same over my shoulder.

They killed too many and would not have stopped.
They won't be seen again.
I'm not proud of ending female lives.
So we'll keep this one between ourselves.
Your faithful servant,
VS

I knew the sisters' strangling days were over as the letter was clearly from the Vigilante Slasher.

"But why did the Slasher only send one pair?" Lottie whispered.

"I assume he kept the other." I gulped.

"Ellen," Lottie asked in a shaky voice. "Who is the Vigilante Slasher?"

"I have no idea," I said, and in that moment, I wished not to know.

I HOPE you enjoyed this book and want to read the next!

Ellen's next adventure follows her as she settles back into life at Ashcombe and eagerly awaits the return of Captain Ernest Hamilton from Cairo. But her peace is shattered when a notorious thief is found dead on the neighbouring Worthington estate. Heading over to console Lady Jane Worthington, a plane crashes on Ellen's land, piloted by flame-haired Alex, the Duke of Loxborough, who is once again masquerading under a pseudonym. As charming as he is, Ellen is unnerved by his presence – she does not trust him.

At Worthington, Ellen discovers that the dead thief had been attempting to steal a pair of rare pink diamonds, recently acquired by Lord Worthington and rumoured to be cursed. Though Ellen would prefer to leave the matter to the police, Jane's pleas – and Alex's insistence on staying in Ashcombe until the case is solved – draw her reluctantly into the investigation. She wants the mystery and Alex gone before Hamilton returns!

If you would like to join my newsletter and read my prequel story to this series then please do so at www.kellymasonbooks.com

ACKNOWLEDGMENTS

I'd like to thank my creative writing tutor Rosemary Dun, both inside the OU and out! You encouraged me to pursue novel writing and gave me so much information and guidance, I'm still reading the handouts! You are amazing. Thanks also goes to my brilliant mentors Alison Knight and Jenny Kane of Imagine Creative Writing and their Novel in a Year course, which gave me lots of help and kept me on track and for continuing to be dear friends.

Thanks to the inspirational friends I met through the Romantic Novelists' Association, and the Bristol writing community (I'm too scared to list everyone in case I miss someone off!) And to my Beta readers, Tara Starling, Cinnomen Matthews McGuigan, and Michelle Armitage. Thanks also to Helen Blenkinsop who is a guru on the 'hook' and amazon ads. And thanks to my best writing friends – Callie Hill, Claire O'Conner and Jenny Treasure, for also being beta readers and for sharing the journey with me. And to my Cozy mastermind, especially Scarlett and my accountability partners Soraya, Halana and Kari. My Editor Becky Halls who is more than an editor and also an inspiration. My final proofreader Liz Lane who hunts for the last pesky typos. And not forgetting my mate Andy who makes life fun! And a huge thank you to Laura who really added a massive dose of inspiration for this particular book ;)

Thank you to my advance reader team who are really supportive and there for me, even from the first book.

Thank you to those on my mailing list who interact with me.

And thank you to Victoria Tait for helping me out so much.

Thanks to my family for supporting me, especially Gary for putting up with me tapping away at the keyboard 24/7.

Made in the USA
Las Vegas, NV
29 March 2025

20266782R00163